* * * * * * *

The night air was cold and still, and the stars filled the sky with tiny specks of light. The faint glow of a half moon provided the only light to see by, dimly lighting the surrounding prairie. The only sounds that shattered the stillness of the night were the occasional wild animal calls of the Sioux warriors who lay in a shallow ravine waiting for the sun to come up.

I rolled onto my back, took in a deep breath as I looked up at the endless darkness. I wasn't sure if the chill I felt was due to the cold night air, or if it was because of the danger tomorrow would certainly bring. Unless some clouds blew in, tomorrow would be bright, sunny, and hot.

* * * * * * *

THE OLD WEST

A COLLECTION OF
WESTERN SHORT STORIES

J.E. Terrall

Best Wishes
J. E. Terrall

ISBN: 978-0-9844591-0-0

This is a work of fiction. Names, characters, and incidents are either a product of the author's imagination or are used fictitiously, and any resemblance to actual persons, living or dead, is purely coincidental.

Printed in the United States of America
First & Second Printing/2008 –   www.lulu.com
Third Printing/April 2010 –   Central Plains Book Manufacturing
                                     Winfield, KS 67156

Covers: Both front and back cover photos were taken by
                 the author, J.E. Terrall

Book Layout/
Formatting: Lynn Eyermann, Scribes Hut,
                 Hill City, South Dakota

THE OLD WEST
A COLLECTION OF
WESTERN SHORT STORIES

To my long time friend
Russ Bailey

CONTENTS

THE BUFFALO WALLOW

The night air was cold and still, and the stars filled the sky with tiny specks of light. The faint glow of a half moon provided the only light to see by, dimly lighting the surrounding prairie. The only sounds that shattered the stillness of the night were the occasional wild animal calls of the Sioux warriors who lay in a shallow ravine waiting for the sun to come up.

I rolled onto my back, took in a deep breath as I looked up at the endless darkness. I wasn't sure if the chill I felt was due to the cold night air, or if it was because of the danger tomorrow would certainly bring. Unless some clouds blew in, tomorrow would be bright, sunny, and hot.

I rolled back over, taking a few minutes to look out over the emptiness of the prairie, and to assess my situation. My mind filled with thoughts of earlier today when my peaceful world came crashing to an end and brought me to this buffalo wallow in the midst of the vast prairie.

* * * *

I had left Kansas City several weeks ago for Fort Morgan on the South Platte River in the Colorado Territory. My plan was to join up with Captain T.J. Sommers of the U.S. Army. Captain Sommers had hired me to guide an expedition across the Rocky Mountains to California.

The day was sunny and hot as I rode across the great prairie. My packhorse plodded along behind with my supplies. I figured that I could make it to the fort in another two or three days.

Shortly after the sun was high in the sky, I noticed tracks in the dirt. I drew up and stepped down from the saddle to study the tracks. They were fresh and were from unshod ponies. There were about eight, maybe ten ponies in all. It was most likely a Sioux hunting party.

Since I was traveling west and the tracks headed north, I didn't figure there was much chance of running into this hunting party. But just to be safe, I mounted up and rode down into a shallow ravine. I traveled along the bottoms of ravines and gullies for the better part of the afternoon, staying off high ground as much as possible to avoid being seen.

By late in the afternoon, I came to a place where I had little choice. I had to travel across a long stretch of open country where there were few places a man could hide. Riding slowly across the prairie to keep the dust down, I stayed alert and ready to make a run for it.

Time seemed to pass slowly as I watched for signs of others crossing the prairie. Letting one's guard down in this vast land of nothingness is a common mistake made by greenhorns. A mistake I should not have made for I am not a greenhorn. I knew the prairie looked flat, but there were often shallow ravines, gullies and small pockets that were not easy to see, but could hide an enemy.

Suddenly, I heard the sound of horses' hooves pounding on the hard, dry ground. I looked over my shoulder in time to see eight to ten Sioux warriors come charging out of a shallow draw at a full run.

This was no place to make a stand and fight. I slammed my spurs into the side of my big gelding and he jumped forward at a run. It was obvious my smaller packhorse would not be able to keep up and was slowing my escape. I cut the lead rope, allowing my packhorse to run free. My gelding quickly pulled away, running at a full gallop. I noticed an Indian turn to chase my packhorse while the others continued to chase me.

My horse was fast and strong. I was confident he would have little trouble outrunning the smaller, less powerful Indian ponies. Leaning down over my horse's neck, I let him run. I could hear the gunshots from behind me and the occasional whistle of a bullet as it whizzed past my head. Suddenly, I felt my horse jerk under me. He stumbled, but managed to keep his footing. I could feel him breathing hard as he tried to keep up the pace, but he was gradually slowing down. A bullet had struck him, but he continued on.

A quick glance back over my shoulder was all I needed. The Sioux warriors were starting to gain ground. It was clear that my horse would not be able to run much farther. I was going to have to make a stand, but where?

As I drew my rifle from its scabbard and levered a round into the chamber, I noticed a buffalo wallow off to the right. If my horse could make it to the wallow, I would have a better chance of making a stand from there.

I turned my horse toward the wallow. As he came up to the edge of it, I reined him in and jumped down. Keeping a tight grip on the reins in one hand and my rifle in the other, I pulled my horse around so he was between the Indians and me. One quick shot through the horse's head dropped him to the ground, providing me with at least some protection.

I quickly lay down behind my dead horse and leveled my rifle. My first shot caught the lead Indian square in the chest and blew him straight back off his horse as if he had been hit across the chest with a heavy board. My second shot caught the second Indian in the right upper shoulder as he tried to rein up and look for place to take cover. He spun around on his horse, then tumbled to the ground. The others scrambled for cover in a shallow ravine.

Everything happened so fast that I had no time to think. I acted entirely on instinct. Now that things had settled down a little, I had time to think and look at my surroundings. I was out in the middle of nowhere with my rifle lying across a dead horse while I waited for a Sioux hunting party to regroup and plan their next move. My prospects of survival were growing dim rapidly. I was outnumbered by at least seven to one, if not more, and I had very few supplies. The only thing I had going for me was that it would be dark soon.

* * * *

Time passed slowly as I waited for dawn. The past few hours I spent taking a mental inventory of what I had while I listened to the coyote calls of the Sioux warriors. I also took some time to consider what my chances might be of getting out of this with my scalp still intact.

If today's weather were anything like yesterday's, this buffalo wallow would be as hot as an oven by noon. With only a little water and little else, my chances of making it through the day were not looking very good. All the Indians would have to do is wait for me to roast under the hot sun.

The thought of a slow death did not appeal to me. I had no desire to just lay there and die in the dirt. The more my mind filled with thoughts of my death, the angrier I became. If I have to die, I'm not about to die alone, I told myself. I would fight to the end and send at least a few of those warriors to the happy hunting grounds ahead of me.

Morning would come soon enough, and I had to figure out a plan that would at least make the odds a little more in my favor. I leaned back against my horse and closed my eyes to think. I tried to remember what the ground around the wallow was like. I remembered that the prairie rolled slightly making it impossible for me to make a run for it on foot without being seen, even at night. I also remembered that the prairie grass was short and very dry for this time of year, providing little cover.

It had not been my plan to fall asleep, but I must have dozed off for a little while. When I opened my eyes, I noticed a slight reddish-orange glow in the sky to the east. It would not be long before the sun would be up. I needed to see what was out there. I rose up on my hands and knees to look over my horse. I slowly scanned the ground around me.

As I looked over the prairie, I noticed something move in the grass. At first, I thought it might be a rabbit or a prairie dog waiting for the sun to rise. Suddenly, I realized that an Indian was crawling through the grass toward me. I raised my rifle to my shoulder and set my sights on him. Slowly, I pulled the trigger back until the hammer slammed down on the firing pin. There was a loud crack and the morning silence was broken.

A loud scream of pain and a cry of anguish filled the quiet morning air. There was no doubt my bullet had reached its mark. Within seconds the air was filled with the sounds of gunshots as the dirt at the edge of the wallow bounced and cascaded over me. I scrambled to the bottom of the wallow trying to make myself as small as possible.

Although it was only a matter of a few minutes, it seemed like eternity before the gunfire subsided. When quiet finally returned, I found myself breathing hard and my face in the dirt. Hugging the ground, I rolled over and looked to see if any of them might have gotten behind me. I saw nothing move.

Slowly, the sun came up over the horizon and began to spread a warm glow over the land. It felt good on my chilled bones, but by afternoon I would be suffering under the sun's increasing heat.

As soon as the sun was full in the sky, I put my hat on the end of a stick and slowly pushed it up above the edge of the wallow. I hadn't pushed it up more than a few inches when my hat flew off the stick just as I heard a rifle shot. Keeping down, I rolled over and picked up my hat. The hole in my hat gave me notice that I had better stay close to the bottom of the wallow, or directly behind my dead horse if I didn't want a bullet in the head. It also told me that at least one of those warriors knew how to shoot, and shoot well.

I lay in the dirt for several minutes just trying to think. There were at least six, maybe seven of them who were in condition to fight. I had shot two at the very start of this skirmish, and one this morning. That meant if I was a betting man, I had little to no chance of getting out of this wallow alive.

In order to keep the Indians from pinning me down so they could move in on me, I would have to exchange a few shots with them from time to time. I waited and listened. The sky had become a royal blue and the air was dead still. Not a sound could be heard. Now was a good time to let them know I was still alive and kicking. I pulled down the lever action of my Winchester and fed another cartridge into the chamber. In my mind's eye, I pictured the place I wanted the shot to go. I took a couple of deep breaths as I tried to ready myself. It would have to be a quick shot - - shoot and duck.

Taking one last deep breath and letting it out, I quickly rolled over, rose up slightly, jerked the rifle to my shoulder and squeezed the trigger. The rifle let out a loud bang and kicked back against my shoulder. Without waiting to see if I hit anything, I ducked back down and hugged the dirt in the bottom of the wallow.

I no more then hit the ground when several shots kicked up dirt around the wallow. I closed my eyes and tried to remember what I saw in the brief second it had taken to make my shot. Out of the corner of my eye, I had seen something move.

At first, I wasn't sure what I had seen. I tried to picture in my head what my eyes had seen. It was then that I realized I had seen one of the others trying to get into a better position to take a shot at me.

I snuggled down near the head of my horse, keeping as close to the ground as possible and keeping my rifle barrel out of sight. I waited patiently for the Indian to crawl around to where I could see him. It seemed to take forever for him to get within rifle shot, but I was ready.

As soon as he saw me, he must have realized it was too late. I already had him in my sights. Before he could get his rifle to his shoulder, the hammer on my rifle slammed down on the firing pin. When the dust cleared, I could see his lifeless body lying in the dirt about fifty yards away. Once again, I had to duck down as bullets hit all around me.

Just as suddenly as it began, it was over. Once again it was quiet. I was sure it would be awhile before they would try to outflank me again. It was a time to wait, and a time to gather my thoughts.

Most of my supplies, including most of my ammunition, were on my packhorse and the Indians had him. I had nothing to eat, only about a half canteen of water, a couple of dozen cartridges for my pistol, and less than a dozen cartridges for my rifle.

However, another problem was beginning to show itself. I was beginning to feel the heat of the sun on my back. It was still early, but it was already getting hot. By noon this sandy wallow would be like sitting in a frying pan. I would be slowly frying like a chicken for Sunday dinner.

I rolled over on my back and looked up at the sky. I had hoped to see a cloud or two, but nothing. There wasn't even a slight breeze to soften the harshness of the sun. It was still a little early for me to worry about the sun killing me. After all, there were several very angry Sioux warriors out there who were hoping to kill me themselves.

The stillness of the morning was shattered every once in a while by a single rifle shot aimed in my direction. I figured the Indians had decided to let the sun slowly bake my brain until I did something stupid, like stand up and fight. I couldn't blame them for playing a waiting game. I would have done the same thing. There is no sense risking any more of their own lives just to kill one man when the sun would do it for them.

By the time the sun was directly overhead, my clothes were wet with sweat. With the sweat, the dirt, the flies, the heat and the stench of my dead horse, I was beginning to feel extremely uncomfortable. I began to think about how nice a bath would feel about now. One like those a man could get out back of the saloon in Kansas City where one of them saloon girls would wash your back, for a price.

I suddenly realized I was losing touch with my situation, and that could be dangerous. I picked up my canteen and took a sip of the warm water. I washed it around in my dry mouth before swallowing it. That little bit of water seemed to help me to think more clearly.

It was again time to let them know I was still here and still very much alive. I levered another cartridge into the chamber and prepared myself for another quick shot in their direction. After a deep breath or two, I was ready. I popped up above my horse, snapped off a shot in their general direction, then ducked back down. I hugged the ground as I waited for them to return fire, but there was no return fire.

I lay in the dirt waiting, but nothing. My head filled with random thoughts. Have they given up, deciding I'm not worth the risk? Did they ride off to get more help? Are they just waiting for me to stick my head up so they can blow it off?

The urge to rise up and look out to see if they were still there was very strong. But no matter how strong the urge, I could not allow myself to take the risk. I lay quietly and looked up at the clear sky. Sweat rolled down my face and burned as it got in my eyes. I was beginning to understand what it felt like to be roasted.

I decided to try the old hat trick again. I put my hat on the end of my rifle barrel and slowly raised it above the carcass of my horse. For several seconds, nothing happened. Either they were wise to me, or they had left. As I lowered my hat, a bullet passed through my hat followed by the sharp crack of a rifle.

"Well, I guess they're still out there," I said out loud as I reached to pick up my hat.

Taking a look at my hat with the bullet holes in it, I could not keep from smiling. I don't know what it was that struck me as being funny. Maybe it was the fact it was so hot that a hat with ventilation sort of appealed to me, or maybe it was the fact my head had not been in the hat when the bullets went through it.

It continued to get hotter as the sun continued to slowly cook me. My lips were becoming parched, my mouth felt like it was full of sand and dirt, and my throat was raw from the lack of water. There is nothing in this world I would enjoy more than to take my canteen of water and dump it over my head. Instead I carefully took another sip of water.

As I was putting the cork in my canteen, a shot rang out and the canteen flew out of my hand. I spun around, drawing my pistol at the same time. My gun jumped three times in my hand as I fired at a figure in the dry grass. When the smoke cleared and the dust settled, I could see an Indian lying only twenty feet or so from the edge of the wallow. It took me a few minutes before my heart rate and my breathing returned to normal. I couldn't figure out why he missed me at such a short distance until I realized he was the same Indian I had wounded earlier. It must have taken all his strength to get close enough to shoot at me. I had to admire his determination, even if he had almost killed me.

Suddenly, shots started to come from the shallow ravine where the Sioux warriors were hiding. At first I hugged the ground, but soon realized the bullets were being fired randomly, with no particular target, just in my direction. It was as if their intention was to keep me pinned down so I could not return fire without risk of being shot.

It was time. They had waited long enough and the time had come to kill me. It is just as well. I don't know how much longer I could last without water and still be able to put up a fight under the scorching sun.

I checked my pistol and rifle, making sure they were both loaded and ready. I crawled up to the edge of the wallow and peeked out. They were apparently in no hurry to die, either. I could see an Indian pop up and take a shot in my direction, then quickly disappear again.

Keeping as low as possible, I continued to watch them. I was sort of hoping one or two of them would get careless and stick their heads up above the grass long enough for me to get a shot at them.

I hadn't noticed it at first, but it seemed to be a little darker as if the sun had gone behind a cloud. At the same time, I felt a hint of a breeze coming from behind me. As I turned to look up at the sky, I felt a sharp, burning pain across the top of my right shoulder followed by the sound of a rifle shot. I knew instantly that I'd been hit.

I rolled down into the bottom of the wallow. The pain was almost unbearable, and I had difficulty moving my right arm. I pulled my neckerchief from around my neck and stuffed it under my shirt to stop the bleeding. The bullet had passed across the top of my shoulder, breaking my collarbone and making it very difficult for me to use my right arm.

Lying back and looking up at the sky as I waited for the pain to subside, I knew my chances of surviving this skirmish were slim. I have never been very good at shooting left-handed, and with the pain, I would be lucky to hit anything.

I lay quietly watching the soft billowy clouds float across the blue sky. The thought passed through my mind that this was a good day to die. Well, no day is a good day to die, but this one would be as good as any, possibly better than others.

My head was so cluttered with thoughts of my bleak situation that it did not register in my mind that the breeze was rapidly turning into a wind. I had completely shut out my surroundings for the few minutes it took for me to get over the first shock of being shot, and to adjust to the pain.

I watched as the clouds began to darken, and the dust from the prairie began to blow. This sudden change in the weather gave me hope.

I rolled back and looked out toward my enemy. I could see several Indians crawling slowly through the grass toward me. Picking up my pistol in my left hand, I aimed at one of them and fired. The bullet kicked up dirt near the Indian, but I missed him. Between the pain in my shoulder and the sweat in my eyes, I wasn't doing very well at hitting my target. At this rate, they would be able to move in close enough to finish me off. Time was running out for me, but I was not ready to give up.

I quickly searched my mind for some kind of a solution, some way to get away or to get them to leave. My thoughts were interrupted by the distant sound of thunder. At the sound, my mind seemed to clear and a plan started to form in my head.

"That's it," I said out loud.

I remembered the wild prairie fires that were often started by lightening. I reached up with my left hand and began to pull at my saddlebag in an effort to get it open. Shots rang out and a bullet struck the edge of my saddle causing me to dive for cover. I grabbed my pistol and fired two quick shots in their general direction in the hope of at least slowing down their advance toward me. I noticed they ducked down quickly, but I knew it would only hold them for a few seconds.

I finally got the saddlebag open and pulled out a small metal box. Retreating back down behind the cover of my horse, I opened the box. Inside was a small amount of tinder, a flint and a piece of steel.

Setting the box down, I crawled to the edge of the wallow and pulled out clumps of dry grass. Using my good hand and my teeth, I was able to take long strands of grass to tie a small bundle of loose grass together. I placed the flint and grass against my horse and began striking the steel against the flint. I tried to light the bundle of dry grass several times, but it would not start. I huddled over it to better protect the bundle of grass from the wind and tried again. Finally, the bundle of grass began to smoke. A thin string of smoke rose from the bundle of grass. I blew softly on it to help it along. The smoke thickened until the grass burst into flames.

I held the burning bundle of grass out and lit the dry grass along the edge of the buffalo wallow. The dry prairie grass began to burn, slowly at first. But as the wind caught it, it flared up and started to spread. Smoke soon filled the air as the wind pushed the fire down the slope toward the Indians. The fire quickly spread out. In a short time, the wall of smoke and flames gained speed as the wind pushed it out across the prairie.

The shooting stopped. The Indians knew what a prairie fire could do, and how fast it could spread. And I knew the fire could turn on me just as fast if the wind should suddenly change direction. It was time for me to get as far away from here as possible, and as fast as possible.

I stood up and looked toward the fire. On the other side of the wall of flames and smoke, I could make out several horses running off in the distance, some without riders. This was no time for me to be standing around to enjoy my small victory. With my injury, and no horse to ride, I would not be able to move very fast.

With a great deal of pain, I tucked my right hand into my belt to help restrict any movement of my shoulder. After holstering my pistol, I picked up my rifle and started off in the opposite direction of the fire.

I knew if I headed due west, I would come to a creek. I could follow the creek to the South Platte River, then up the river to Fort Morgan. Once I get to the creek, I would have water and shelter from the scorching sun all the way to the fort. The trees and brush along the creek and river would provide places where I could hide should I come across another Sioux hunting party.

It would probably take me three or four days to get to the fort, but once I got there I would be able to get my shoulder treated by the Army Surgeon. The expedition would be delayed in leaving, but I was still alive.

JUSTICE IN ASTORIA

Two men rode into the small prairie town of Astoria. Their clothes were covered with the dirt and dust from a long hard ride. A single point of a sheriff's badge peeked out from under the duster of one of the riders giving the only clue as to who these men might be. They rode up in front of the livery stable and sat in their saddles for a moment as they looked the town over.

Astoria wasn't much of a town. There was only one road that seemed to run endlessly across the prairie without so much as widening out for the town. The buildings were faded and weather-beaten from the hot summer sun and the harsh cold winters of the Dakota Territory. The few randomly scattered houses also showed the results of the extreme weather conditions.

"Can I help you gents?"

The two men turned and looked down at the large stocky man standing in front of them. He wore a thick leather apron covered with scorch marks and soot. He held a heavy hammer in one hand, while in his other he held a large set of tongs with a red-hot horseshoe clamped tightly in its jaws.

The tall lean rider dismounted and stood in front of the blacksmith and said, "We're looking for five, maybe six men that might have passed through these parts a couple of days ago."

"Well, mister, I don't know if they're the ones you're lookin' for, but six men rode into town the day 'for yesterday."

"Was one of them shot up?" the husky dark haired rider asked.

The blacksmith looked up at the rider before replying. "Yeah. He's over at Doc's, and not doin' so good."

"Where are the others?" the tall lean rider asked.

The blacksmith turned his back to the riders and dropped the hot horseshoe into a bucket of water. The water hissed and bubbled as steam rose from the bucket.

"Couldn't say for sure, but I'd guess they'd be in the hotel or saloon. Won't be hard to find 'um," he added as he turned back toward the riders. "We only got one hotel and one saloon."

"We'd like our horses rubbed down, fed and watered, and put up for awhile."

"That'd be two bits a piece."

The two riders tied their horses to the hitching post, then paid the blacksmith. After removing their saddlebags and rifles, they started down the street.

The blacksmith watched them as they headed toward the sheriff's office. He'd seen lawmen like these two before, but not in recent years. They were hard men with deep-rooted values, strong wills and the determination to complete the task they set out to do.

When the two men entered the sheriff's office, they found him sitting at his roll top desk with his feet up. The sheriff jerked his feet off the desk and swung around in his chair.

"Howdy, gents. Somethin' I can do for you?" he asked, as he looked them over.

"I'm Jess Bowman, sheriff from Pierre. This here's Stan Sanborn, sheriff from Blunt."

"I'm Sheriff Will Parker," he replied as he stood up and shook hands. "What brings you so far from home?"

"We've been tracking six men," Jess said.

"That's a far piece to track someone. What'd they do?"

"They escaped from the brig at Fort Thompson, robbed the bank in Pierre, and shot a woman and her kid down in the street. Then they rode east to Blunt where they robbed a store and killed the owner," Stan explained.

"Now, you understand I don't take to no man that kills women and kids, but you don't have no jurisdiction here."

Jess's eyes narrowed and the muscles in his neck tightened. He wasn't about to let these men get away because some cow town sheriff was more concerned about jurisdiction than justice.

Stan quickly stepped up alongside Jess and nudged him lightly on the arm. He knew Jess's temper better than anyone, and this sheriff was pushing his luck with Jess.

"You don't seem to understand, sheriff," Jess said clinching his teeth in an effort to control himself. "I'm not asking for permission, or your help. We'll take care of them ourselves."

"Now, you look here," Sheriff Parker said forcefully. "I don't want no trouble in my town. They ain't done nothin' again' the law here."

"No, you look," Stan interrupted, the expression on his face turning hard. "You already have trouble. We've tracked these killers half way across this territory. If you're not going to help, then you best stay out of the way?"

Sheriff Parker had noticed how these lawmen stood and how they held their rifles. It was easy to see they meant what they said. It was clear to Sheriff Parker that anyone who did get in their way might end up in a pine box alongside the men they were after.

Stan could see on Sheriff Parker's face that they had made their point and there was no need to say anything more. Stan nudged Jess to get him to back out of the office.

Jess didn't take his eyes off Sheriff Parker as he slowly backed out the door while Stan stood calmly staring at the sheriff. Once Jess was outside, Stan backed out to the street. They turned and walked across the street toward the hotel.

Sheriff Parker let out a sigh of relief as soon as they were gone. He knew these two lawmen were as dangerous as the outlaws they were after. He quickly convinced himself that this was a good time to leave town for a while.

Jess and Stan walked across the street to the hotel. Just before entering, they stopped to look up and down the street. The street was empty. They turned and stepped into the hotel. Jess went to the desk to register while Stan stood near the door where he could keep an eye on things.

The desk clerk got up as soon as he saw them come in. He took a second to look them over before stepping up to the desk.

"We'd like a room on the street side," Jess stated.

"Put your mark here," the clerk said as he held out a pen.

Jess laid his rifle down across the counter and took the pen. The clerk turned the register around and watched Jess as he signed his name.

"That'll be a buck," the desk clerk said as he handed Jess a room key.

While Jess was checking in, Stan stood back in the corner and kept his eyes moving. He looked past the double swinging doors into the hotel bar, but it was empty except for the bartender and a man sitting at a table playing solitaire.

When Stan looked into the parlor, he noticed a woman sitting at a table writing a letter. He took note of the young woman because of the dress she was wearing. It was rather fancy for this part of the country. It was not only pretty, but it fit the woman's curves as if designed just for her. The woman was obviously from a big city. Stan wondered what a woman like her was doing here in this shabby little town.

"Let's go," Jess said disturbing Stan's thoughts.

Stan followed Jess up the stairs. As they turned down the hall, Jess stopped and glanced at the first door he came to. Stan was about to say something when the door opened, and two men stepped out into the hall. The four men eyed one another as if sizing each other up. Stan and Jess were both quick to notice the guns that they were wearing.

"You looking for somethin', mister?" the larger of the two men asked in a harsh deep voice.

The one who spoke was a little larger than average. The long scar on the side of his face gave him a sinister, almost evil look. His clothes were typical of most cowboys, except he was wearing U.S. Army cavalry boots.

"Just looking for our room," Jess answered casually.

"Well, this ain't it, buster," the man replied as he turned and walked down the hall followed by the smaller man.

Jess nudged Stan and looked down at the floor. Stan looked down at the smaller man's feet and noticed he was wearing cavalry boots, too.

"There's two of 'um'," Jess whispered.

Stan nodded in agreement. As soon as the men had gone down the stairs, Jess and Stan walked on down the hall to their room.

Once inside the room, Jess set his rifle next to the door and tossed his saddlebags on the end of the bed. He walked over to the window, pushed the dingy curtains back and looked out. From the window he could see the sheriff's office and the general store with the doctor's office above it. He couldn't see the saloon or livery stable as they were on the same side of the street as the hotel.

"From the descriptions of the men who escaped from the fort, the two in the hall were Art McFinney and his brother, Donny," Stan said as he dropped his saddlebags in the corner.

"I was just wondering. You think that we can get them separated so we don't have to deal with all of them at once," Jess said as if he was simply thinking out loud.

"It's possible."

"There's one in the doc's office across the street," Jess added. "We need to find out where the others are."

"You could have a drink right next to them and they wouldn't know who you are, but I can't. Siltz and Walker know me from a run-in we had in Blunt about a year or so ago. If they see us together, they'll know why we're here."

"You're right," Jess agreed.

Just then, Jess saw Sheriff Parker come out of his office. He had a small box in one hand and a fishing pole in the other. Jess watched as the sheriff hurried down the street toward the livery stable. Within a minute or two, the sheriff came riding out of the stable and on out of town.

"Well, that takes care of Sheriff Parker. Looks like he's goin' fishin'."

Stan got to the window just in time to see Sheriff Parker disappear behind a building at the edge of town. He took a moment to look around. Stan suddenly pulled back away from the window.

"What's the matter?"

"There's Siltz," Stan said as he pointed toward a man walking down the steps from the doctor's office.

Siltz was a rather slim young man with narrow hips and straight shoulders. His wide brimmed hat was pushed back on his head allowing Jess to get a good look at his face. He was clean shaven and didn't look to be any older than about sixteen.

Even though Siltz was young, Jess had heard of him and knew him to be as quick and deadly as a rattlesnake with a gun. His gun was slung low on his hip and tied down on his leg like the gunfighters Jess had read about in dime novels. The gun looked to be a Colt, typical of those used by the Army and not the best for a fast draw. But Siltz had perfected the fast draw with it pretty well and was not to be underestimated.

"You stay here and keep an eye out. I'm going to the saloon and see what I can find out," Jess said as he moved away from the window."

Jess left the room and went down to the lobby. A quick look around assured him there was no one in the lobby except the woman standing near a window with her back to him. She was holding the curtain open and seemed to be busy watching something out on the street.

Jess stepped out onto the wooden walkway and looked up and down the street. It was getting on toward noon and the street was quiet with only a few people going about their business. Jess looked around for Siltz, but he had already disappeared.

Looking down the street, Jess saw a man sitting in a chair in front of the saloon. The chair was tilted back against the wall near the saloon door. The man had his hat tipped forward over his eyes. His pants were a faded blue with a slightly darker blue strip down the leg. It was easy to see the gold colored stripe that usually ran down the leg of the Army uniform pants had been removed. He was also wearing cavalry boots like the others. Even with his hat covering his face, Jess was sure the man was Matt Filmore, another of the escapees.

So far, Jess and Stan had been able to identify four of the six men. That left only two, Bill Walker and Jeb Miller, the leader of this bunch. Jess was sure that Walker was the one he shot as they made their escape from Pierre. He was a little surprised that Walker had lasted long enough to get this far.

Jess glanced up toward the window of the doctor's office. If Walker were in good enough condition to sit or lay near a window, he would have a good view of the street. That could prove to be a problem later on, Jess thought.

Jess turned and walked toward the saloon. As he passed the hotel window, he noticed the woman was no longer there.

When Jess reached the saloon, Filmore raised his head and glanced up at Jess. Jess froze in his tracks until Filmore tipped his head back down, showing no interest in him.

Jess looked inside the saloon. The McFinney brothers were standing at the bar drinking beer. In the back corner was a large man sitting at a table playing with a deck of cards.

Jeb Miller had dark wavy hair and a thick black mustache. His eyes were narrow set and appeared cold and hard. He had a thin cigar in his teeth; the smoke from it was getting in his eyes and forcing him to squint. He tilted his head to one side as he played with the cards.

Sitting beside Jeb was a young woman wearing a dress like the ones worn by saloon girls in the larger towns, but her dress was old and worn. She watched as Jeb played his game, but she didn't seem to take any interest in it. Jess had seen women like her before, women who sold themselves then were mistreated by the men paying them.

Jess stepped into the saloon and moved directly to the end of the bar. Everyone turned to look at him, which made Jess's nerves tingle and his senses sharpen. Jess felt like he had walked into a den of wolves and he was their next meal.

The bartender moved to the end of the bar and asked, "What'll yah have?"

"A beer."

The bartender drew a beer and set it on the bar in front of Jess. Jess put a coin on the bar and picked up the glass. As he took a sip of the lukewarm beer, he scanned the room. Jess didn't want any surprises.

"What brings you to these parts, mister?"

Jess took in a deep breath to ready himself for whatever might happen, then slowly set the glass on the bar and turned toward Jeb. Jess knew the ways of men like these and noticed the little things other men often missed, things that could cost them their lives.

The first thing Jess noticed was Jeb had the playing cards in one hand, but his other hand was under the table. He also noticed that the McFinney brothers were still at the bar, but they had set their beers down and were standing upright rather than leaning casually against the bar. It was clear to Jess that this was not the time to get into a gunfight.

"Cattle, mister," Jess announced with a big grin. "You got any to sell?"

"No," Jeb replied laughingly. "There ain't a lot of cattle around here. These are mostly dirt farmers around here."

"I'm not looking for just any cattle," Jess countered quickly. "I'm looking for breeding stock, good hardy breeding stock. I heard there's some good stock up this way, so I come here to find out."

Jeb looked across the room at the McFinney brothers, then at the girl sitting next to him. It was clear that Jeb was trying to decide if Jess was really a cattle buyer.

Jess watched Jeb for some indication of what he had decided. As Jeb slowly drew his hand out from under the table, the McFinney brothers turned back to the bar. Jess turned back around to the bar and picked up his beer. He took a long slow drink in an effort to calm his tense nerves. When he finished his beer, he set the glass on the bar and walked out of the saloon.

As Jess stepped out on the walkway, he let out a sigh of relief. If they hadn't believed him, it could have turned into a bloody shoot-out. He suddenly remembered that Filmore had been sitting in front of the saloon. A quick glance at the chair revealed that Filmore was gone. Jess looked up and down the street, but there was no sign of him.

Jess returned to the room and told Stan about his encounter with Jeb Miller. He also told Stan he was positive that it was Walker who was shot up and in the doctor's office.

"Shortly after Siltz left the doctor's office, one of the others went up," Stan said. "I think it was Filmore. Looks like one of them is staying with Walker all the time."

"That means we only have four left. If we can get them split up, we have a good chance to get all of them.

"When do we start?" Stan asked.

"As soon as it's dark."

* * * *

Jess spent the afternoon looking out the window and planning their next move. The sun was setting and the shadows had grown long on the ground. It was time to get ready. Jess shook Stan, waking him from his nap.

"What's up?" Stan asked as he sat up.

"Time to get up. Let's go have dinner," Jess suggested as he rose up from the window ledge.

"But what if I'm seen?"

"Siltz is back in the doctor's office with Walker. None of the others know us. Besides, I just saw the McFinney brothers heading toward the hotel."

Stan followed Jess out of the room and down the stairs. As they entered the dining room, Stan noticed the young woman, again. She was sitting at a table in the corner eating dinner, alone. She glanced at Stan, but quickly looked away. Stan wondered what a classy lady like her was doing here. She looked like a woman of means, certainly not a poor dirt farmer's wife. She didn't seem to belong here.

Jess noticed her, too, but his interest was in the two men who were just sitting down. He had been right. The McFinney brothers had come back to the hotel for dinner.

Jess nudged Stan and directed him to a table next to a window. Jess sat down so he could watch the McFinney brothers, while Stan sat so he could watch the street.

A rather large woman wearing a white apron came out of a side door and walked over to the table where Jess and Stan were seated.

"Can I help you gents?"

"Hey, you. We was here first," Art McFinney called out rudely.

The expression on the woman's face quickly turned from a pleasant smile to a blank, cold stare as she turned and looked at the McFinney brothers. She looked like she wanted to say something about their rudeness, but quickly changed her mind.

She turned back and looked at Stan and Jess. "I'm sorry. I didn't know they came in first."

"That's all right."

"I'm sorry. I'll be right back."

Jess nodded, then glanced over toward the McFinney brothers. The look on Donny's face showed how proud he was of his big brother's ability to bully people. Jess would like to wipe the stupid grin off Donny's face, except this was not the time. Jess could wait to see the look on Donny's face when he is arrested along with his big brother.

The woman sitting at the table across the room finished her dinner, then got up and left. Stan watched her as she turned and went up the stairs.

"It doesn't look like anyone else is coming to dinner," Stan whispered.

"Be ready. I'll take Art, you take Donny as soon as the waitress gets out of the way," Jess whispered.

As soon as the waitress had taken their orders and returned to the kitchen, Jess stood up and started across the room as if he was going to look at a painting hanging on the wall. Just as he stepped next to McFinney's table, he tipped the table over, knocking over the glasses of water.

Art McFinney tried to curse, but everything happened so fast that the words never came out. As he and Donny pushed back away from the table to avoid getting wet, Jess drew his gun and lunged straight at Art. He pushed his gun in Art's face as he shoved him back against the wall, tipping over his chair and crashing to the floor.

At the same time, Stan drew his gun and shoved it in Donny's face, catching them both off guard.

"Not a sound or it will be the last sound you make," Stan said as he looked into Donny's wide, surprised eyes.

"You'll never get away with this. We got friends," Donny said defiantly.

That was the last thing Donny said. Stan hit him across the side of his head with the barrel of his pistol.

"Now what? We can't take them to the jail. We'll be seen from the doctor's office," Stan said.

"We'll take them to their room and tie them to the bed. That should hold them until we have the others."

Jess grabbed Art by the collar, pushed his gun under Art's chin as he jerked him up off the floor. He could see the hate in Art's eyes.

"One wrong move from you and you'll be as dead as the woman and kid you shot down in the street."

"I didn't kill no woman."

"You might as well have, you was a party to it," Jess said as he pushed him toward the door.

Stan pulled Donny up and pitched him over his shoulder like a sack of potatoes. Once inside McFinney's room, Jess and Stan hog-tied and gagged the two brothers. After making sure they were secure, Jess and Stan returned to the dining room.

The waitress came out of the kitchen and approached the table where Jess and Stan where seated. She was carrying two large plates piled high with steak and potatoes.

"I seen what you fellahs done. You two lawmen?"

"Sort of, but you don't need to tell anyone," Jess replied with a pleasant smile.

"I won't. I won't tell nobody," she said as she set the plates in front of them. "You fellahs eat up, it's on the house. You'll need a good meal under your belts if'n you're goin' after them others."

About halfway through the meal, Stan stopped and looked out the window. Jess wondered what was going through his mind.

"Yah know, I think you should walk down to the saloon and arrest Miller and Filmore," Stan said without so much as turning back to look at Jess.

"Okay. You got an idea as to how I should go about it?"

Stan turned around, looked across the table at Jess and began explaining his plan between bites. Jess listened as he finished his dinner. Stan's plan had a few flaws in it, to say the least, but it was better than anything else they had going for them.

When they finished their dinners, Jess stood up and looked down at Stan. He thought about saying something about their years of friendship and how much that friendship meant to him, but decided to just go and get the job done.

Jess turned, walked out of the hotel onto the walkway. He stood for a moment as he glanced up at the window of the doctor's office, then turned and started toward the saloon. The distance to the saloon was less than sixty feet, but it seemed like the longest and loneliest walk he had ever taken. The sound of his boots echoed in his ears with each step.

When he reached the saloon, he stopped at the window and peeked in. Miller was sitting at the far end of the room. The girl who had been with him earlier was nowhere in sight.

Filmore was leaning on the bar with his hands wrapped around a mug of beer. He was talking to the bartender and laughing. From what Jess could see of the rest of the saloon, it was empty.

He let out a sigh of relief as he drew his gun from its holster and checked it to be sure he was ready. After holstering his gun, he took in a deep breath before stepping through the saloon door.

Filmore turned and looked at Jess as he walked through the door. Having seen Jess earlier in the day, he made no effort to ready himself for a confrontation. He simply turned back toward the bartender and began talking again.

Miller had straightened himself up in his chair when he saw Jess come in the saloon. Jess noticed that Miller had casually slipped his right hand down under the table. The move gave notice to Jess that Miller was still not sure if Jess was really a cattle buyer.

"Well, there. Did you find any critters?"

"Yap, as a matter of fact I did. I found two real nice bulls on a farm a little east of here," Jess replied as he walked over to the table and stood in front of Miller.

"Pull up a chair," Miller said as he withdrew his hand from under the table.

"Sure."

Just as Jess was reaching for the chair, Filmore called out to him. "Don't I know you?"

Jess froze in his tracks as his muscles tensed and his heart raced. Whatever happened now was going to prove to be tricky. Jess didn't remember ever running into Filmore before, but then anything was possible. Filmore could have seen Jess when he passed through Pierre while in the Army, or he might have recognized Jess when they exchanged shots after the bank robbery in Pierre.

Jess slowly turned around to face Filmore. Filmore was leaning back with his elbow on the edge of the bar. Jess was relieved to see that Filmore was not in a position to make a fast move for a gun.

"I don't think so," Jess said as casually as possible.

"I remember where I've seen you before," he said as he pushed himself up and started to position himself.

Jess couldn't take the chance of letting him get set. He had to act before he had both men to deal with. Jess quickly stepped sideways and pushed hard against the table, pushing Miller and the chair he was sitting in over backwards, dumping Miller on the floor against the wall. Jess drew his gun and fired a shot at Filmore as he dove for cover behind a table.

Jess's shot went wide, but it gave him time to get off another shot before Filmore could recover from the sudden confusion. The second shot caught Filmore flat-footed, hitting him square in the chest and knocking him back against the bar. Filmore fell to the floor as his knees buckled.

Before Jess could turn and see where Miller was, two quick shots rang out. One hit the floor near Jess's face throwing dirt and wood splinters in his face. He didn't know where the other shot went. For a second, Jess was unable to see, but he heard the sound of something dropping on the floor.

When he cleared his eyes of the dirt, he saw Stan standing near the back of the room with his gun pointed at Miller. His eyes moved to Miller's lifeless body lying on the floor with his gun still in his hand. Stan had come in through the back door of the saloon in time to get Miller before he could kill Jess.

"Thanks," was all Jess could manage to say as he took a deep breath.

"You all right?" Stan asked.

"Yeah, I think so," Jess said as he stood up and looked around the room. Both Filmore and Miller were dead.

When it was over, the dance hall girl came down the stairs. The expression on her face was one of surprise when she saw Miller lying dead on the floor. She looked up at Jess, then walked to the bar. Picking up a damp cloth, she stepped up in front of Jess and carefully began wiping the dirt from his face.

"Thank you," she said softly. "He was mean."

"No, thank you."

Jess found the girl to be compassionate and pretty. He couldn't help but think that under the right circumstances, she would make someone a good wife.

Suddenly, Jess's thoughts were interrupted.

"Art, everything okay in there?"

"Everything's just fine, Siltz. Why don't you come on in?" Stan replied.

Before anyone could move, a shot ran out and a bullet crashed through the front window of the saloon. Stan and the bartender dove for cover, but not Jess. The girl had grabbed Jess around the neck and was leaning against him as she looked up at him with eyes that were big and glassy. The stray bullet had hit her in the back. Jess wrapped his arms around her and gently lowered her to the floor. She looked up at him and smiled. Slowly, her eyes closed and her body went limp.

"I'll go out the back. You keep him busy," Jess said as he stood up.

Jess rushed out the back door of the saloon and around to the side of the building. He cautiously worked his way along the side of the building. When he got to the front corner of the building, he could hear Siltz yelling at Stan.

"Sheriff Sanborn, I didn't expect to see you this far from home. It's nice to run into you again."

"I knew we'd meet again, someday," Stan yelled back.

"I'm sure you did, but this time I have a gun and you don't have any friends. I saw the sheriff leave town."

Stan could hear the slight chuckle in Siltz's voice. There was no telling what Siltz might do. Everyone knew he was a little crazy and a lot dangerous.

"By the way, Siltz, you're on your own, too. Miller and Filmore are dead, Walker is in no condition to help you, and the McFinney brothers are tied up."

In the excitement, Jess had forgotten about Walker. The mention of his name caused Jess to look up toward the doctor's office across the street. The dim moonlight reflected off something near one of the upstairs windows. It took Jess only a second or two to realize the moonlight was reflecting off a rifle barrel, and it was pointed toward the front of the saloon. It was obvious that Walker was not out of the fight, yet.

Jess took careful aim at a spot very near the barrel. Slowly, he pulled back the hammer of his gun and gently squeezed the trigger. The hammer slammed down and the gun bucked in his hand. There was a cry of pain and a rifle tumbled out the window, falling to the ground in front of the general store. Just as quickly, there was the sound of gunshots and flashes of light from the dark shadows in front of the general store. Jess hugged the side of the building as several bullets ripped through the corner scattering small pieces of wood all over.

In among the loud sounds of gunfire, there was the distinct sound of a small caliber pistol. One single shot, then silence.

The sound of such a small caliber pistol seemed to catch everyone by surprise. Jess knew Stan never carried anything other than his Colt .44. Siltz was not known to carry any kind of a small pistol, and all Jess ever carried, other than a rifle or shotgun, was a .45 caliber Colt Peacemaker.

The silence seemed to last forever, although it was only for a minute or two. Carefully, Jess peeked out from around the corner. He saw a figure moving in the shadows near the building.

To Jess's surprise, Siltz slowly walked out of the shadows into the light. He had a blank stare on his face and his arms hung loosely at his sides. He held his gun in his hand, but he made no attempt to raise it, or point it at anyone. Siltz staggered a few steps as if drunk, stopped, then fell flat on his face in the dirt.

Slowly, Jess stepped out of the darkness into the light from the saloon windows. Stan came out of the saloon and stood beside him as they looked down at Siltz. They heard a noise coming from next to the general store and quickly raised their guns.

A shadowy figure stepped out of the darkness into the light. It took them a second or two to believe what they were seeing. It was the same young woman they had seen in the hotel. She walked toward them carrying a small caliber pistol in her hand.

She looked down at the dead man in the street for just a second, then at Stan. She held out the pistol to him. "I guess you will want this," she said politely.

Stan reached out and took the gun from her. She just stood there looking at him as if she expected him to do something.

"I'm ready."

"Ready for what, Ma'am?" Jess asked.

"I'm ready to go to jail for what I've done."

"I'm not goin' to put you in jail."

"But you have to. I killed a man, and you're the sheriff."

"I'm sorry, ma'am, but we don't have any jurisdiction here," Jess said with a smile as he realized how ridiculous his words sounded.

"I don't think you will be going to jail. You shot a man who killed a woman and child," Stan explained.

"He killed my brother six months ago in Omaha," she said softly.

"I'm sorry, but it's over now. You go back to Omaha," Stan said. "Justice has been served, even if not according to the law."

"Thank you," she said as she gave a slight hint of a smile to Stan.

Stan and Jess watched the woman as she walked back toward the hotel. They both knew this woman, whoever she was, had probably saved at least one of their lives.

"What do you say we get our prisoners locked up? We can start back home in the morning," Jess suggested.

Stan glanced back over his shoulder in time to see the woman disappear into the hotel. He wondered who she might be. Maybe, if he saw her in the morning, he might introduce himself and find out her name.

For Jess, it was enough to simply let her go, knowing that justice had been served.

PAWNEE STATION

The sun was scorching the already dry prairie. It hadn't rained for weeks and the buffalo grass that covered the prairie for as far as the eye could see was brown and withered. Every afternoon the sky would cloud up and the wind would blow, but the rain would not come to make the prairie green again.

I was still forty miles north of Fort Morgan on the South Platte River. My horses were showing the effects of doing without adequate water and a good helping of oats. It had been a long time since I'd had anything to eat, too. I'd found it necessary to use my water sparingly.

Shortly after I passed Pawnee Buttes, I saw a few trees off in the distance. Where there were trees, there was often water. If my information was correct, the building in among the trees would be Pawnee Station.

Pawnee Station was not much more than a sod house that served as a trading post and stagecoach stop for the run between Julesburg to the east and Fort Collins to the west. I'd heard a man named Frank Mills ran the station.

As I rode toward the station, I noticed a column of smoke rising from a small butte to the east. This was the third or fourth time in the past couple of days I'd seen smoke from signal fires. It was clear that trouble was brewing, but just what kind of trouble I couldn't say.

I kept an eye toward the column of smoke as I nudged my horses along. I noticed another column of smoke further to the east, but it was different. It was thick and dark like the smoke from a burning house or barn, nothing like the white smoke from a signal fire. It was too far away to tell what was burning.

The smoke from a burning building and smoke from signal fires could mean only one thing. Some Indians had gone on the warpath. It all kind of made sense when I took time to think about it. I'd heard rumors at Fort Robinson that buffalo hunters had been down this way. The word was they slaughtered a herd of buffalo and took only the hides and tongues, leaving the carcasses to rot in the sun. I hadn't seen any sign of buffalo hunters, but this was a big country. Up until now, the only things I'd seen were a couple jackrabbits.

It was almost noon by the time I got to Pawnee Station. I drew up a good distance from the sod house to take time to study the place. At first it looked deserted, but off to the right was a corral with six horses in it. It was clear they had recently been fed. The trough was full of water and the horses were feeding on loose hay. Off to the left was a fresh grave.

Looking back at the sod house, I noticed a thin ribbon of smoke coming from the chimney. As my eyes drifted to one of the windows covered with heavy wooden shutters, I noticed the end of a rifle barrel poking out a small peephole. I discovered another rifle barrel sticking out of the other window. The sight of rifles pointed in my direction tends to make me nervous.

"Anybody home?"

"Don't move, mister. We've got our guns on you. One move and we'll shoot."

The voice was that of a rather nervous woman. I wasn't about to do anything that might make her nervous enough to shoot.

"Yes, ma'am. Just take it easy," I said as I slowly raised my hands up so the woman could see they were empty.

"Who are you? What do you want?"

"The name's Sam Grover. I'm on my way to Fort Morgan. I was hoping to get some water and feed for my horses, and maybe, something for myself."

I sat in my saddle and waited. I was having a hard time trying to figure out what it was about me that made them take so long to decide if it was safe to open the door. I noticed one of the rifle barrels disappeared from a window. Seconds later, I heard the door being unbolted. As the door slowly opened, I took a deep breath and let out a sigh of relief.

"You can't blame us for being a mite bit careful," the woman said. "We've been seeing a lot of smoke signals lately."

"I've seen them, too," I replied. "You mind if I get down, ma'am? I've been in the saddle a long time."

"Oh, I'm sorry. Please, get down. You can put your horses in the corral. There's plenty of feed and water for them. As soon as you're done, come inside."

"Thank you, ma'am," I replied as I dismounted.

I walked my horses to the corral. While I was taking the gear off my packhorse and stowing it under the shelter of a lean-to, I heard movement behind me. I dropped what was in my hands and swung around, drawing my gun as I turned.

I suddenly found myself face to face with a girl. I must have surprised her, as her eyes were as big as saucers as she stared down the barrel of my gun. Seeing this pretty young girl was a bit of a surprise to me, too.

"You shouldn't come up behind a man like that, Miss. You could get yourself shot," I said as I relaxed and holstered my gun.

"I'm sorry, mister. I was just coming out to see if I could help with the horses."

"Okay. You can take this one and give her a drink and something to eat, if you like. She's kind of a glutton, so don't let her drink too fast."

She smiled as she reached out and took the reins. I watched her lead the horse into the corral. If I had to guess, I would say the girl was about sixteen or seventeen years old. She had long blond hair and beautiful blue eyes. She was the prettiest thing I'd seen in a long time. Her smile could capture the heart of a man faster than he could hog-tie a calf. There was no doubt the girl under that plain cotton dress was really a young woman. I shook my head in an effort to get my mind back to what I was supposed to be doing.

I took the saddle off my horse and set it on the ground, then walked him into the corral. As I stood beside my horse while he drank, I glanced over at the girl and caught her watching me.

"What's your name?" I asked.

"Jessica, Jessica Mills," she said with a big smile.

"Well, Jessica, you think we can leave the horses now and go back to the house?"

"Sure."

I took the bridles off the horses and left them to eat. Dropping the bridles over my saddle, I picked up the saddle and started toward the house with Jessica walking beside me. We didn't talk. Just walking beside her gave me feelings inside I hadn't felt before. Even as tired as I was, I still managed to walk straight and tall.

When we got to the door of the house, I dropped my saddle over a bench on the porch and opened the door for Jessica. Stepping inside, Jessica's mother turned and looked at us.

"Just in time, Mr. Grover," she said with a smile. "Please, sit down."

I sat down at the table and looked around the place. The house wasn't much, but it was clean and seemed to be quite comfortable. Everything seemed to have a place and everything was in its place. In one part of the room, there were shelves stocked with canned goods and a few staples that could be purchased by anyone passing by. Along one wall was a large stone fireplace that served as part of the kitchen area. It most likely served as a source of heat during the winter. It must have been the smell of the woman's cooking that made the place feel so much like a home.

My thoughts were interrupted when Jessica's mother set a plate of steaming hot venison stew on the table in front of me. After setting a plate in front of Jessica, she served herself.

"It's nothing special, but I think you'll like it," she said as she sat down at the end of the table.

"Thank you, ma'am," I said as I looked at the first real food I'd seen in days.

"I guess we forgot to introduce ourselves. I'm Rebecca Mills and this is my daughter, Jessica."

"I met Jessica out at the corral. Nice to meet you, ah, Mrs. Mills?"

"Yes," she replied softly.

I thought I saw a bit of sadness come over her face, but she recovered quickly and forced a smile. Her reaction to my calling her "Mrs. Mills" gave me cause to wonder.

"We don't get much news out here, Mr. Grover. Do you know what's going on? Why all the smoke signals?"

"I heard some rumors when I passed through Fort Robinson that there's some Indians that might be going on the warpath. It seems some buffalo hunters slaughtered a herd of buffalo for their hides and left the carcasses to rot. I guess I can't blame the Indians for being a mite upset over that.

"Off to the east, I saw a bit of smoke that wasn't from a signal fire. The smoke was too dark, most likely a house, or barn, or something like that, would be my guess."

"The only thing east of here for twelve miles or more is Logan's Station, one of the stage stops," Rebecca said as a worried look came over her face.

"That could be the place."

Jessica glanced at her mother, then looked across the table at me. Her eyes slowly turned down as she scooped up a spoonful of stew. It was clear she'd seen the worry in her mother's eyes, too. It was then that I remembered the grave I'd seen when I rode up.

"Excuse me for prying, ma'am," I said as I tried to pick my words carefully. "I couldn't help noticin' a grave out there just past that old cottonwood. You mind telling me who's buried there?"

Rebecca looked at me while her eyes filled with tears, then she stood up and went outside without saying a word. I looked across the table at Jessica. Rebecca's reaction confused me, and caused me to wonder if maybe I'd said something I shouldn't have.

"My father's buried there, Mr. Grover," she said quietly.

"I'm sorry. I didn't know."

"That's okay. It's been kind of hard on mother."

"I'm sure it has, but what about you?"

"I'm okay. Father took sick way last fall. We tried to get him to go to Fort Collins on the stage to see a doctor, but he said a doctor wouldn't be any help. I miss him a lot.

"Before he died, he helped me to understand a little about dying, and about life. We'd sit and talk late into the night after he got so sick he couldn't get around.

"Mother managed to stay pretty strong right up until he died, then she sort of fell apart for awhile. We buried him by the old cottonwood a week ago."

"What's she going to do now?"

"I don't know. Mr. Webber, Nate, should be here in a day or two. Maybe he'll think of something. I think he'd like to take father's place, right here. I think he's sweet on mother. I think she likes him, too."

"Don't you think that's a mite bit soon?"

"Maybe to some folk's way of thinking. He's been helping us ever since father first got sick."

I quickly realized this young woman was mature far beyond her years. This was a hard land with people that were few and far between. Out here when you made a friend, you worked hard to keep that friend. It was a place where companionship was as important as love.

My thoughts were interrupted by a movement in the doorway. I glanced over to see Rebecca slowly backing into the house. She was watching something that I couldn't see from the table.

"What's the matter?" I asked.

"There's a wagon coming, and something's wrong," Rebecca said as she stepped back inside the building.

"What makes you say that?" I asked as I got up and moved to the door.

"Nate would never push his team that hard on a day like this unless something was very wrong."

I reached down and picked up the rifle I'd left next to the door. Stepping outside, I saw the wagon coming toward us kicking up a lot of dust. I swiftly scanned the horizon, but I saw nothing that would give the driver reason to push his team so hard.

As the wagon drew close, Nate pulled back on the reins, pushed hard on the brake arm with his foot and yelled at the team to stop.

"Whoa! Whoa!

The horses almost skidded to a stop as Rebecca came out of the house.

"What's the matter, Nate?" Rebecca called out.

"Got an injured man in the back," he replied as he wrapped the reins around the brake arm and jumped down off the wagon.

"Bring him inside. Jessica, get some water," Rebecca ordered.

I noticed Nate took only a second to look at me as he rushed to the rear of the wagon. I got the impression he was more than a little interested in who I was and why I was here, but he didn't say anything.

I helped him move the injured man inside. We put him down on a daybed in the corner of the room and stepped back out of the way. I could see the man was seriously hurt.

Jessica set a pan of water and some cloth next to the bed. Rebecca wet a piece of cloth and looked down at the injured man. She took a deep breath as she realized she knew him. She turned and looked up at Nate with a shocked look on her face.

"This is Sam Logan," she said with surprise.

"Yes, ma'am. His place was burnt down last night or early this mornin'. All the horses was gone, too," Nate explained.

"What about his family?" Rebecca asked.

"The boy and his ma were dead. I couldn't find the girl," Nate said almost apologetically. "I didn't have time to go an' hunt for her. I was afraid the same thing might happen here, so I rushed over."

Jessica sat down near her mother holding a hand full of clean rags to use for dressings.

"We're all right, Nate," Jessica assured him.

"From the looks of Logan's Station, I - - ," Nate stopped talking and looked at me when I nudged his arm.

"I think we should go outside while the womenfolk tend to Mr. Logan," I said.

"Yeah, sure," Nate replied realizing that sometimes it is better not to say too much.

I followed Nate to the door. Once outside, we walked over to the wagon and leaned against it.

"Name's Sam Grover."

"Nate Webber," he replied as he stuck out his hand.

I shook hands with him and noticed he had a strong grip. Something about him made me think he could be depended on if we had to fight.

"I thought it best we talk away from the womenfolk. There's no sense scaring them anymore than they already are."

"I agree. Which way'd you come in from?"

"I came down from the north, from Fort Robinson. I haven't seen anything except smoke from several signal fires and smoke from another fire off east."

"That'd be Logan's place."

"I guessed that."

"What do we do now?"

"You said something about the Logan girl missing. Do you think she was taken by the Indians?"

"I sure enough do. She was a right nice lookin' girl, only fourteen."

"Got any idea where they might have taken her?"

"Don't know for sure," Nate said as he rubbed his beard. "But from the tracks they left, I'd say they was headed up along Wild Horse Creek. There's several places up that way where they camp from time to time. Say, you ain't thinkin' of goin' after her, are you?"

"You got a better idea?"

"Well, no. But it sure is risky."

"After dark, you get Logan and the women in the wagon and head south to Fort Morgan. Be careful. When you get to the fort, find Captain Summers and tell him where I am."

"Okay, but I think you're crazy to go after the girl alone."

"You may be right about that, Nate."

* * * *

The afternoon was sticky and hot, and passed by slowly. The clouds grew big and threatened rain. It did rain a bit, but not enough to even settle the dust. A breeze came up for a little while, but it grew calm again in the evening as the sun began to set.

Nate and I took up positions where we could see out over the prairie. Nate was near the corral where he could watch to the south and west, while I sat under the big cottonwood so I could watch to the north and east.

The sun set in a blaze of colors. As it grew darker, the outline of the mountains to the west became faint against the skyline and finally disappeared. A coyote howled off in the distance and an owl hooted in a nearby tree.

My mind was filled with thoughts of what I was planning to do. I knew I would have just one chance to find and rescue the girl. If I couldn't find her tonight, we might never find her.

I vaguely remembered crossing Wild Horse Creek earlier in the day. It was about ten miles straight north. Once I found the creek, I would have to decide which way to go to find their camp, and hope I picked the right direction.

My thoughts were suddenly disturbed by the sound of something moving in the grass behind me. I eased my hand down over my pistol grip and slowly drew my gun while I listened in an effort to figure out who might be there. Just as I was about to make my move, I detected the faint smell of coffee and decided it had to be Jessica, or her mother. Slowly, I slid my gun back into my holster and glanced over my shoulder.

"You shouldn't sneak up on a man."

"I know, but I thought you might like some coffee," she said as she stepped around in front of me and held out a cup.

I looked at her as I reached up for the cup. I could see her outline in the dim light of dusk. There was something different about her. Maybe it was the way her voice sounded, or the way she smiled at me. It wasn't until she sat down under the tree that I noticed she was wearing pants and a shirt, and she had her hair tied back.

"They're getting the horses ready for us," she said casually as she looked out into the darkness.

I wasn't sure I had heard her correctly.

"What do you mean, 'us'?"

"Nate said you're going after Molly Logan. You will need help with the horses."

"No, Jessica. I'm not taking you along. It's too dangerous."

"You can't go alone."

"And just why not?"

"You don't know where the Indians are camped."

"Neither do you."

"True, but with two of us looking we have a better chance of finding them. Besides, you'll need someone to help with the horses. You won't be able to keep them quiet by yourself. I can do that for you.

"Nate can't go to help you. He has to stay here and help mother get Mr. Logan in the wagon and drive it to Fort Morgan. Mother can't go 'cause she needs to take care of Mr. Logan. That leaves me."

As much as I didn't like the idea, she made a lot of sense. It wasn't as if she didn't know how hard life could be out here, she grew up on the prairie. Reluctantly, I gave in.

"Okay, you can go, but at the first sign of trouble you get yourself back here, and fast. You understand that?"

"Yes," she replied with a grin of satisfaction as she leaned against my shoulder. "When do we leave?"

"In about an hour or so. As soon as the moon comes up."

* * * *

Time passed quickly with Jessica leaning against me, her head on my shoulder. I could smell the delicate fragrance of her hair. I felt comfortable with her beside me and didn't want to disturb her, but it was time.

I woke Jessica and got to my feet. After I helped her up, we walked to the corral. Three horses had been saddled and tied outside the corral. Nate was leaning against the corral with Rebecca at his side.

"Good luck," Nate said as he handed my rifle to me.

I slid the rifle into the scabbard, then mounted. I reached down and took the reins of the extra horse from Nate.

I watched as Rebecca handed a gun to Jessica, then kissed her on the cheek.

"I hope you don't need this, but your father would want you to have it."

Jessica strapped the gun belt around her waist and mounted up. She looked at me as if she expected me to say something, but I had already come to expect the unexpected from her. There was no doubt in my mind that she knew how to use a gun.

We turned the horses and started to ride north. I glanced back over my shoulder and saw Nate with his arm around Rebecca's shoulders as they watched us ride off into the darkness. We rode at a slow, but steady pace. It would take us awhile to get to Wild Horse Creek and we didn't need tired horses when we got there.

When we were getting close, we stopped, dismounted and walked the horses to the edge of a slight rise overlooking the creek. In the moonlight, we could make out the trees along the creek. It was an eerie sight. The trees were just black outlines and cast faded shadows on the prairie grass.

We looked up and down the draw in an effort to decide which way we should go. The creek was almost dry due to the long period without rain. If the Indians were camped on this creek, it would most likely be where the creek had more water in it. Jessica must have been reading my mind.

"I think we should go along the draw to the east," she whispered. "There's a place not far from here that usually has more water in it. They might be camped there."

I motioned for Jessica to lead the way. We mounted up and rode at a walk down off the top of the rise toward the creek. When we reached the creek, we turned and rode east in the shadow of the trees.

We had gone about two miles when I noticed a flicker of light ahead of us. I reached out and touched Jessica on the arm. She stopped immediately and looked at me. I put my finger over my mouth to make sure she didn't speak, then pointed toward the light.

"Looks like it could be a campfire," I whispered as I stepped out of the saddle.

She nodded in agreement and stepped down from her horse.

"You wait over there in that ravine with the horses," I whispered. "I'll check it out. If any shooting starts, stay there as long as you can, but don't risk getting caught. If they come this way, get out of here as fast as you can, and find your mother and Nate."

"What about you?"

"I'll find my way to Fort Morgan and meet you there."

She again nodded that she understood. I started to leave when she reached out and grabbed my arm. I stopped and looked back at her. Her eyes sparkled in the moonlight, yet I could see sadness in them.

"You be careful, Sam Grover," she whispered, then leaned toward me and kissed me lightly on the lips.

I was surprised by her kiss, but maybe a little more surprised by my own reaction as I kissed her back. Suddenly, I didn't want to leave her, but I knew what I had to do. I turned and started moving along the creek toward the light.

I found the Indians camped in a small grove of trees along the edge of the creek. Sneaking in among the trees, I was able to work in close enough to see the camp. The fire had almost burned down to coals and was giving off just enough light for me to see what was near the fire. I counted four of them sleeping near the campfire. There hardly seemed to be enough of them to be considered a war party. It made me wonder if there might be more of them lurking around. However, the possibility that we'd found the wrong Indians also crossed my mind.

I heard a noise back in the bushes. At first, I wasn't sure what it was. It sounded like a small animal crying, but I quickly realized it could be a girl crying. Then I heard what sounded like someone clapping, or slapping someone followed by a muffled cry of pain, then silence.

Keeping down, I crawled among the bushes and trees toward the sounds. As I came around a bush, I froze. Not twenty feet in front of me was an Indian with a rifle cradled across his arms. He was guarding the horses, but his attention was distracted by Molly's whimpering. I slowly backed under the bush before he had a chance to see me. I held my breath. When the Indian didn't make a move, I let out a silent sigh of relief.

I lay on the ground and peered out from under the bush. I could make out seven Indian ponies and several larger horses. The larger horses were probably from Logan's Station. If I was correct, that meant there were seven Indians. I made a mental count, four sleeping by the campfire, the one guarding Molly and the one guarding the horses. That meant there was one more.

Suddenly, a pair of moccasins appeared beside me on the other side of the bush. I could feel my heart pounding in my throat. I waited breathlessly as he slowly moved passed. He stopped only a few feet from me and looked toward where Molly was being held prisoner.

Taking a deep breath, I reached down and carefully slipped my knife out of the top of my boot. As the Indian turned his back to me, I stood up and grabbed him from behind. I quickly put my hand over his mouth to prevent him from calling out, then used my knife to silently send him to the happy hunting ground. I quickly rolled him under the bush before the guard could see me. It wouldn't be long before he would be missed, so I had to move fast.

I tried to quiet the horses as I moved among them, but the smell of a stranger made them nervous. The Indian who had been guarding the horses turned and looked around to find out why the horses were so nervous. In the darkness, and with the horses between us, he couldn't see me. I darted across the clearing and back into the brush.

I watched from my new hiding place while the Indian calmed the animals and scratched his head while he tried to figure out what had upset them. When I was sure it was safe to move again, I retreated deeper into the bushes.

Moving silently among the trees, I found Molly. The moonlight gave me no clue to her condition. I could see her hands were tied behind a tree, and she was kneeling on the ground. In that position, the circulation to her legs would be restricted and it would be hard for her to jump up and run once I cut her free.

The Indian who was guarding her must have lost interest in torturing her. He was sitting on the ground leaning against a tree some ten to twelve feet away.

This presented me with a problem. If I tried to get Molly out of the clearing, the commotion would wake the guard. If I killed the guard first, Molly might get excited and call out for me to help her, alerting the others before we could get away. The longer I waited to do something, the greater the chance the others would miss the one I had already killed.

Using the cover of the undergrowth, I crawled around until I was directly behind Molly. Keeping low, and keeping Molly between me and the guard, I slowly moved up behind her. I reached around from behind and put my hand over her mouth. She tried to scream, but no sound escaped from her lips.

"Shhhhh. I'm here to help you," I whispered softly. "Don't say anything, don't make a sound. I'm going to cut you loose, but don't move," I instructed her, then removed my hand from over her mouth.

I hoped she was a sensible girl and understood the situation. When my knife cut through the rope, she did as she was told. Even though her hands were free, she kept them behind her back.

"Keep an eye on the guard. When you see him fall over, duck back here in the bushes and wait for me. You understand?"

"Yes," she whispered softly.

I drew back to the cover of the bushes and began working my way around to where the guard was sitting. I crept up behind him and grabbed him from behind. I quickly and quietly ended his life.

I glanced across the clearing to see if Molly had done what I had told her to do. She was gone. I let out a sigh of relief.

Suddenly, there was a call of alarm. I was sure they had found the body I left under the bush. It would only be a matter of minutes before they would be searching for us.

I ran across the clearing and dove into the bushes. I grabbed Molly by the arm and pulled her deeper into the cover. We stumbled into a patch of bushes where we could hide until I got my bearings. I pushed Molly down under the bushes and slid in beside her.

We could hear the Indians as they talked and argued. I drew my gun and waited as I tried to think of what to do next. I knew that to stay here would mean certain death, but it would be better to die fighting than to give up.

I could sense Molly's fear even though I couldn't see her face in the darkness. The only thing we had going for us was that they didn't know how many of us there were.

Just as suddenly as it had begun, the talking and the noise stopped. We had waited too long. They had gotten over the first shock of someone being in their camp, and the death of one of their own. They were starting to search for us.

I realized it wouldn't take them long to search the small grove of trees and brush that surrounded their camp. We were going to have to make a run for it and take our chances in the open. Our only hope was to find a draw or ravine nearby that would provide us with cover.

"Come on," I whispered as I grabbed Molly by the arm and pulled her out from under the bushes.

As soon as we were both on our feet, we began running out across the prairie. Molly stumbled in a hole and fell, crying out in pain. I grabbed her, pulled her to her feet and began running again. As we came to the top of a rise, we heard the crack of a rifle shot quickly followed by several other shots.

Suddenly, I felt a sharp pain in my side and stumbled to the ground. I knew I had been hit and wouldn't be able to run. I looked up and saw Molly just standing there looking down at me.

"Go that way," I said as I pointed toward where Jessica would be waiting with the horses.

"Run, run," I yelled.

Molly turned and began running. As soon as she was gone, I turned and prepared to provide cover for her escape.

In the darkness, I could just barely make out four or five non-descript figures carefully moving up the ridge toward me. There was the occasional flash from a rifle barrel and the sound of shots being fired. As carefully as possible, I took aim at the figures and fired back. It was too dark to see if I hit any of them, I just fired in an effort to pin them down, and hopefully slow their advance.

As suddenly as it began, the shooting stopped. I knew it would be just a matter of time before they would creep up on me. The silence of the night was eerie. The pain in my side was beginning to burn like I'd been stuck with a hot poker. I couldn't see my wound so I had no idea how badly I was hurt, but I knew I was going to need help soon, or I would die right here.

Out of the corner of my eye, a shadowy figure holding a rifle loomed up in the darkness. I quickly turned and fired at the figure. It folded and fell to the ground. Just as quickly, I heard several shots to my right and turned in time to see two dark, shadowy figures fall. I realized the shots came from someone on my side, and that could only mean Jessica had come for me. Jessica was at my side in seconds, holding me tightly to her in her arms.

"You shouldn't have come back for me. You have to get out of here."

"I'm not leaving without you."

This was no time to argue with a woman with her persistence and courage.

"Can you walk?"

"I think so," I replied as she slipped her arm around me and helped me to my feet.

Once I was standing, I leaned against her as she led me along the bottom of the ravine where she had left Molly and the horses. Molly was holding them and trying to keep them quiet.

Jessica helped me to my horse and gave me a boost into the saddle. I hung onto the saddle horn with both hands while I waited for Molly and Jessica to mount up.

"Can you ride?" Jessica asked.

"I'll have to."

"Let's get out of here," she said.

We kicked our horses in the sides and they took off across the prairie at a full run. We heard a couple of shots from behind us, but our horses quickly put us out of sight and out of range of the Indians.

When we arrived back at Pawnee Station, Jessica and Molly helped me into the house. Jessica cleaned and dressed my wound while Molly kept watch at the window.

While Jessica and Molly refreshed the horses for the ride to Fort Morgan, I had a chance to lie on the bunk and think. Jessica was a fine young woman and would do a man proud. Once this trouble with the Indians settled down, I'd like to come back here with Jessica and make a home for us, if she'd have me.

Jessica came back into the house and smiled at me as she crossed the room and sat down on the edge of the bunk.

"You feeling better?"

"Yes. Jessica, can I call on you when this is over?"

"After all we've been through, Sam Grover, you darn well better," she replied with a big grin, then leaned down over me and kissed me.

"But right now we'd better get going."

SACRED LAND

GOLD! GOLD!

The Sioux Indians had known that gold existed in the Black Hills for a very long time. Word of the precious metal was leaked out to the white man's world by fur traders, missionaries and a few others who had contact with the Sioux. Although it had been known for many years that there was gold in the Hills, the rush to the Hills to find it did not occur until after George Armstrong Custer's Military Expedition to the Black Hills in 1874. Only a few miners had worked their way into the Black Hills in search of the yellow metal prior to Custer's Expedition.

The Black Hills were a sacred land to the Sioux Indians. Over the years they did their best to protect the Hills from outsiders, but the white man kept coming in numbers too great for the Indians to stop. Many of the miners who came to the Hills in search of gold in those early days never returned to their families, and were never heard from again. This is the story of two such miners, Jacob Miller and Fred Summerfeld.

* * * *

Jacob led the two pack mules cautiously along a narrow deer trail through the tall Ponderosa Pines. On one side of the trail was a jagged rocky cliff towering high above him. On the other side was a wooded slope that dropped into a long narrow meadow below. A shallow creek wandered slowly through the meadow.

Dark clouds rolled across the sky warning of an impending storm. The distant sound of thunder echoed through the wooded canyons and made the mules nervous and jumpy. Jacob held the mules' reins tightly in an effort to control the animals as he tried to keep them moving.

Suddenly, Jacob froze in his tracks as he looked into the meadow below and noticed an Indian ride out of the trees on the other side of the creek. He was all too aware of what the Indians did when they caught a white man on their sacred land. He quickly gathered the mules in close behind a large boulder and crouched down.

"Easy there, fellah," Jacob said softly as he tried to keep the animals quiet.

As he watched, five more Sioux warriors rode their ponies out of the trees and down to the creek for a drink. Several of the Indians knelt down beside their ponies to get a drink, too.

One of the Indians must have heard the clicking of hooves on the rocks from the nervous mules. The Indian stood up next to his pony and looked up along the rocky ridge. He spent several minutes scanning the trees and rocks for a clue as to what had made the sound that he had heard. He mounted his pony, nudged him across the creek and began to move closer to the rocks where Jacob was hiding.

Jacob calmly drew his pistol from its holster and laid it on the boulder, just in case he might need it quickly. Carefully, he lifted his rifle and laid it across the boulder. Tucking the butt of the rifle into his shoulder, he aimed it at the curious Indian. Slowly, he pulled back the hammer as he waited and watched the Indian over his rifle. He was ready to fight for his life.

A shiver went through Jacob as his eyes looked on the face of the Indian. It was almost as if they had made eye contact, but they were too far away from each other. He could not understand the feelings that he was experiencing. It was as if he knew this Indian from another time or another place. Jacob could not remember a time in his life when he felt this nervous and frightened, yet he had an overwhelming desire to know this man.

Jacob found himself studying the Indian very intently and wondering what the Indian was thinking. The Indian was a young warrior with a strong lean muscular build. His skin was dark, and his long black hair neatly braided giving him a look of royalty. Yet, the two yellow stripes of war paint under each eye on his high cheekbones gave him a savage look. He wore moccasins and a loincloth, and carried a bow and a quiver with a number of arrows in it. His bow seemed to be rather long and thin by Sioux standards, yet Jacob was sure that it was a good bow. The bow had a single white and brown eagle feather tied to the tip of it. His pony also had a matching feather tied to the bridle.

The movement of the other Indians suddenly distracted Jacob's thoughts. He could see they had finished and were mounting their ponies. An older warrior, who carried a long spear with several feathers and several small pieces of hair hanging on it, called out impatiently for the young warrior to come back.

"Gray Wolf, come," he called in Lakota, the language of the Sioux.

Reluctantly, Gray Wolf turned and rode back to join the others. He kept turning and looking back over his shoulder toward the ridge. He had heard something in the rocks, but it could have been a deer.

Jacob breathed a sigh of relief as the Indians started moving off down the meadow. It was not until that minute that he realized how nervous he had become. Sweat rolled down his face and he was breathing rapidly. He holstered his pistol while still watching them.

Jacob waited in among the rocks until he was sure the Indians had gone, then he started moving the pack mules along the trail again. He moved along as quickly as possible, but continued to watch back over his shoulder. He wanted as much distance between him and the Sioux warriors as possible.

A quick look up through the trees at the sky told Jacob that he would most likely get wet before he could get back to camp with the supplies. If it rained, the trail would become slippery and travel would be difficult.

"Come on, you darn fool mules. We gotta get a movin'," he said as he pulled on their reins.

Jacob kept thinking about the young warrior. He could not get it out of his head that he knew this Indian, but he could not think of how that was possible. The one thing he seemed to be sure of was that he was destined to see Gray Wolf again.

The first few drops of rain soon turned into a downpour. Within minutes the narrow deer trail was turned into a ribbon of mud, slippery and wet. The mules were reluctant to push forward, but Jacob pulled on the reins and coaxed them along.

The sound of thunder continued to come closer and closer. Suddenly, there was a bright flash of light and the sharp crack of thunder. A nearby tree exploded, sending branches and limbs flying, and splitting the tree in half.

Startled, the mules jumped and pranced around. Jacob tried to hold them, but one of the mules broke free and ran wildly down the narrow trail with supplies being scattered along the way. The frightened animal was soon out of sight.

Jacob managed to hang onto the other mule and was able to calm the animal. There was little he could do about the one that ran away. Jacob cursed the mule. He knew if it were found by the Indians, it would be just a matter of time before they would come searching for him and his partner.

The rain was cold and coming down hard. There was no time to worry about the mule now. He had to get back to camp with what supplies were left. Jacob pulled and tugged on the reins of the mule and started up the trail toward camp. There was no doubt in his mind that Fred would be madder than hell over the loss of the mule and the supplies, but there was nothing Jacob could do about that now.

It took well over four hours for Jacob to find his way back to the camp in the pouring rain. When he arrived, he discovered the camp was deserted. Although everything was there, the fire in the cook stove was out and the flap of the tent lay wide open. A quick look around the camp told him that Fred had not packed up and left, so what could have happened to him? It was not like Fred to be panning for gold in this weather.

Fred had grown lazy after weeks of panning and finding only small amounts of color. It had gotten to the point where Fred would not even do his share of the work around the camp. As a result, their relationship had become strained.

Jacob thought of calling out for Fred, but that would not be wise. He didn't know if there were Indians around, and it was best to keep quiet. The thought that Indians may have taken Fred passed through his mind.

He tied the mule to a nearby tree and drew his rifle off the pack. Pulling the hammer back, he began working his way through the trees and brush to the creek where they had been panning. As Jacob stepped out of the trees onto the rocky bank of the creek, he looked around. There was no sign of Fred, but he heard strange noises coming from downstream. He stepped back into the trees.

Being as quiet as possible, he worked his way through the trees along the bank until he came around a bend in the creek. The closer he got to the noises, the stranger the noises sounded. It sounded like people talking, rather mumbling, but he could hear the sound of only one voice.

Jacob spotted Fred squatting down in the creek. Fred was cursing and digging frantically with his hands in the bottom of the creek, throwing water and gravel in all directions.

Suddenly, Fred stood up and raised his hands to the sky. As he looked up, he cried out, "I got yah. I got yah."

Jacob could not see what Fred was holding in his fingers, but it was clear that Fred had found something, probably a gold nugget. He started to move from the cover of the trees, but months of hiding from the Indians told him to use caution. Jacob scanned the surrounding area before stepping out on the bank of the creek.

"Fred, what'd yah find?"

Fred swung around and stared at Jacob for a second before he quickly closed his hand over the gold nugget. "It's mine. I found it. It's mine," he yelled.

Jacob had never seen Fred like this before. His eyes were big and glassy. His face was contorted and had an evil look. They had been friends for years and had always shared with each other, but Jacob suddenly realized that he no longer knew this man.

"What's yours?" Jacob asked calmly.

Fred looked from Jacob's face to the rifle he held loosely in his hand. Without warning, Fred drew his pistol and pointed it at Jacob. Jacob stumbled back a couple of steps before he regained his balance.

"Drop the gun," Fred demanded.

"What's wrong with you?"

"I said, "Drop the gun"."

Jacob realized that Fred had lost all control of himself. Reluctantly, he dropped the rifle in the sand. He had heard about people reacting strangely to finding gold, but he never expected it from his lifelong friend. Fear gripped Jacob as he looked at the gun Fred pointed at him.

"Turn around," Fred demanded.

Jacob hesitated for only a second, then did as he was told. As he slowly turned around, he closed his eyes and said a silent pray that his old friend would not shoot him in the back.

"This gold is...is...mine."

Jacob heard the pained sound in Fred's voice as the last words he said faded away. He turned and looked over his shoulder and saw Fred reaching for his back with one hand as he staggered in the creek. There was a look of agony on his face, and he reached out toward Jacob just before falling face down in the creek. Jacob saw the arrow sticking out of Fred's back.

Jacob froze for a second, but the sight of Gray Wolf stepping out of the trees on the other side of the creek brought him back to reality instantly. Jacob quickly turned and darted back into the trees. He did not try to recover his rifle, he simply ran for his life.

Several other Sioux Warriors came out of the trees and stood in the creek watching as Gray Wolf took his knife and swiftly removed the hair from the head of the intruder to their sacred ground. Holding it high in the air, Gray Wolf let out a blood-curdling scream.

Jacob could hear the victory cries of the warriors, but he did not look back. He knew that it would not be long before they would be on his trail. His only hope was to put as much distance between them as he could.

He ran wildly, crashing through the tree branches and the brush. Several times he slipped in the wet ground and fell in the mud, only to scramble to his feet and run again. He did not feel the branches as they slashed at him, cutting his clothes and scratching his face and arms. The fear of a slow and painful death was all that kept him going, but that alone could not keep him running forever.

He came to a steep slope that dropped into a stream. He tried to stay on his feet, but fell and slid down the embankment rolling into the cold water of the stream. Grasping a fallen tree, he pulled himself up and hung on.

Jacob's heart was pounding so hard and so fast that he could feel it as well as hear it. Each breath he took was painful as his lungs gasped for air, and his body ached.

He listened for the warriors that he was sure would be following him, but heard only the sounds he himself was making. He hung onto the tree as he tried to catch his breath. Slowly, he began to think more clearly. He began to think of how he might get away, how he might have a chance to live. He made a silent pray asking the Lord to help him find a way out of the Black Hills.

Gradually, Jacob began to gather his senses. He reached for his pistol only to discover that his holster was empty. He had lost his gun in his effort to escape. He was sure he had left an easy trail for the Indians to follow, and it would not be long before they would find him. It was clear that he could not stay here. If he were going to survive, he would have to find a place to get dry and to hide for the night.

Jacob let go of the tree and floated down stream, being as careful as possible not to leave any signs in the stream that the Indians could follow. He did not know how far he had traveled when he came to a rocky overhang that would provide him with some shelter. He discovered a shallow cave where he could build a small fire to keep warm and dry his clothes. It was almost dark by the time Jacob had settled in and was beginning to feel a little safer.

* * * *

After Gray Wolf had scalped the first intruder, he waded across the stream. He bent down and picked up the rifle that the second intruder had left in the sand. He studied the rifle for a minute, then looked off in the direction that the intruder had gone. He turned around and handed the rifle to one of the warriors. He said something to his friend, then walked off to follow the trail that had been left by the intruder.

The other warriors did not follow Gray Wolf right away. There was plenty of time for that. Instead, they rummaged through the camp. They took those things they could use and destroyed everything else. One of the Indians found the small cache of gold the miners had panned over the months they had worked there. It did not amount to much. When they were satisfied that everything the white man could use had been destroyed, they set out to follow Gray Wolf and search for the other miner.

It was an easy trail for Gray Wolf to follow as fear had made the intruder run, throwing caution to the wind. This was nothing new for Gray Wolf because he had tracked down many other intruders who had come to the Hills in search of the yellow sand. Yet, this man was somehow different. Gray Wolf was not sure why, but he knew that this man was not like the others.

Gray Wolf found where the intruder had slid down the embankment into the stream, but he was not sure which way he went from there. It was getting dark and the trail would be impossible to follow.

It was only a short time before the others joined him. They set up camp by the stream to wait for the morning light.

* * * *

Jacob woke to the sounds of birds in the nearby trees. It was a refreshing sound. He rubbed the sleep from his eyes and looked out across the stream. There was a slight fog hanging over the stream, but the sun would soon burn it off.

As he sat up, he realized that he was hungry. He thought about trying his hand at fishing without a pole, but he knew that he did not have time. The Indians would soon find him if he did not move on.

Jacob crawled out of the shallow cave and carefully moved down to the stream. After a drink of cold water, he turned and started north along a narrow rocky ridge. He followed the ridge as it wondered away from the stream in the hope that the Indians would not be able to follow him over the rocks. As he moved along, he kept looking back to see if he was being followed, but saw nothing.

The rocky ridge gradually rose above the stream, then turned to run generally in the same direction as the stream. There were several places along the ridge where Jacob could see the stream twist and turn a hundred feet or so below. At one point he thought he saw something moving along the edge of the stream, but he was not sure. At another outcropping, he saw two Indians walking along the edge of the stream as if looking for something. Jacob was sure they were looking for tracks where he might have come out of the stream. He felt a bit safer knowing that they were a hundred feet below him and did not know where he was.

Climbing on an empty stomach was hard. It was mid-morning and he had to stop to rest. Jacob walked over to the edge of the ridge and looked down. He could still see the two Indians moving along the stream in the same direction as he was going.

Suddenly, he caught sight of something moving out of the corner of his eye. He ducked down behind a fallen tree, then looked back along the ridge where he had been. Fear gripped his heart when he saw Gray Wolf running at a slow but steady pace along the ridge with his long bow held loosely in his hand.

Jacob looked for others along the ridge, but saw no one other than Gray Wolf. He studied the movement of Gray Wolf as he jogged along the ridge. Jacob wondered how Gray Wolf knew that he had taken to the ridge to make his escape.

The longer Jacob watched Gray Wolf, the more he felt they had something in common. Jacob could not remember ever seeing Gray Wolf before, yet he felt a kinship with him. Somewhere deep in the back of his mind, he knew they were destined to clash. He had known it from the first time he had seen Gray Wolf.

Gray Wolf had nothing to go on except intuition. Although the others had chosen to stay along the stream in search of the intruder, Gary Wolf followed his head. Something inside told him that the intruder would take the high ground instead of following the stream that would take him to the Belle Fourche River, and to safety.

In the past, many other intruders had been caught because they chose to follow the stream to the Belle Fourche River. Gray Wolf, although he did not understand it, knew the intruder was not like the others. He was clever and would not be easy to catch. It would take all the skills that Gray Wolf could muster to capture him.

Jacob realized Gray Wolf would catch up with him soon if he continued going in the same direction. He looked around and noticed a shallow draw that went off in a different direction. The draw was full of bushes and brush. It would be difficult moving through the brush, but it would provide cover.

Keeping as low as possible, Jacob scurried across the rocky ridge and into the brush. Being careful to leave no signs for Gray Wolf to follow, he crawled on his hands and knees as he worked his way deep into the thick cover. He lay on his stomach to wait and watch. He could see the rocky ridge through the lower branches of the bushes. As he waited, he could hear his heart beating in his chest. Fear was once again gripping him and causing him to breathe in short, quick breaths.

He lay silently in the dirt as Gray Wolf stopped less than twelve feet from him. Jacob held his breath as Gray Wolf knelt down and studied the ground. Sweat ran down his face and stung his eyes, but he could not allow himself to move. It was certain death if he was discovered.

It seemed to take forever before Gray Wolf was satisfied that Jacob was not around. Jacob thought of trying to jump out of the bushes and attack Gray Wolf, but Gray Wolf would see him before he could get out from under the brush. Gray Wolf was also much younger and stronger. Fear was the reason for not attacking him, the fear of dying.

When Gray Wolf finished studying the ground, he looked back at the draw before he began to follow the rocky trail along the edge of the ridge. Gray Wolf sensed that something was different as he continued his pursuit of the intruder, but he could not figure out what it was. It was almost as if he knew that he had lost the intruder's trail, but the intruder was a white man. He would never think to go deeper into the Hills rather than take the quickest route to safety, or would he, Gray Wolf wondered.

As soon as Gray Wolf had disappeared, Jacob began looking around for a new trail to follow. This Indian was smart and had out-guessed him at every turn, so far. It was time to change his plans.

Jacob crawled out of the brush and started off into the deep woods, away from the ridge and the stream. He kept low as he moved through the dense undergrowth at the very edge of the woods. The further into the woods he got, the less undergrowth he found. It made it easier for Jacob to move quickly. He ran in an effort to put as much distance between himself and Gray Wolf as possible.

Jacob found that he tired easily as he had not eaten since early yesterday. He soon realized that if he stood any chance of escaping, he would have to find something to eat. He came upon a large patch of berry bushes. If he spent too much time in one place he risked being seen or even captured, but he had to have something to eat. He quickly grabbed at the bushes pulling berries off and stuffing them in his mouth as fast as he could. While he ate, he kept watch for any sign of movement in the trees.

The berries not only provided him with nourishment, but with much needed liquid. He knew that if he ate too many berries he could get a stomachache, but he had to risk it.

He had taken his last handful of berries and was about to leave when he saw a movement out of the corner of his eye. He dropped down behind the bushes. His mind raced as he looked around for an escape route, but there was none. He was sure that this was the end. He could hear the soft sound of moccasins on the dry leaves not more than ten feet away.

The time had come to face his enemy. He knew he could not outrun him, and it was better to die fighting than to die the slow, painful death of a captive.

Slowly, the sounds of footsteps moved closer to him then stopped. He rose up carefully to see over the bushes. Only a few feet in front of him was one of the warriors with his back to him. It was not Gray Wolf, but that mattered very little. It was now or never. Picking up a rock, he jumped up and rushed the Indian. The Indian turned just as Jacob got to him, but it was too late.

Although the Indian tried to protect himself, Jacob's hand with the rock in it came crashing down on the side of the warrior's head. The two of them fell to the ground with Jacob landing on top of the Indian. In his frightened state, Jacob hit the Indian again and again. When the Indian didn't move, Jacob rolled off him and looked down at him.

A sense of victory washed over Jacob, he had beaten his enemy. But as he began to realize what he had done, fear gripped him again. What little chance he had to escape with his life was now gone. Now that he had killed one of them, they were certain to hunt him down and kill him. He would be given no mercy.

He looked to see if any of the others were around. Although he was sure that they were, they had not seen him yet. He rolled the body under some bushes and quickly pushed brush over it.

Jacob was trying to decide which way to run when he heard a coyote call. He knew it was not a coyote, but the Indians slowly closing in on him.

He took the knife from the dead Indian before he stood up and began to run again. He heard the piercing scream of a warrior coming from behind him. He knew immediately that he had been seen and that he was once again running for his life. He ran recklessly through the woods. Although he could not see them, he knew that there were several Indians chasing him. He could hear their screams as they pursued him.

As he ran past a tree, an arrow shot past him and stuck into a tree. He crashed through low branches and jumped over fallen trees as he ran. Just as he turned to see how close they were, an arrow pierced his leg. He grabbed at his leg in pain, fell to the ground and rolled several feet. He dragged himself behind a bolder and leaned up against it. He knew it was over. He could not run anymore, so he waited for them to come and finish him off.

Gray Wolf heard the war cries of his friends and came running. He knew that they had found the intruder, but he did not want them to kill him, not yet. He wanted to see his enemy up close, to face him before he died. When he arrived, his friends had the intruder cornered and were waiting at a distance.

Jacob lay against the bolder, waiting. Sweat rolled down his face and his chest pounded. He held the knife tightly in his hand. He could not see the Indians, but he could hear them. They were all around him. They stayed hidden in the brush, making wild animal sounds to make sure he knew they were close.

Jacob waited for what seemed like forever, but they did not come to kill him. What were they waiting for? Why didn't they come and finish him off? Were they afraid of him?

The injury to Jacob's leg made his leg feel like it was on fire. He closed his eyes and tried to will the pain away as he rubbed his leg. Suddenly, it was quiet. There were no more animal calls, no birds making noises in the trees, just dead silence.

Slowly, he opened his eyes and looked up. Standing not more than fifteen feet in front of him was Gray Wolf. Gray Wolf stood with his long bow stretched back ready to let the arrow go. Jacob felt a strange feeling come over him. It was as if he sensed that a friend had come to him in his final minutes of life. There was no fear or panic in Jacob, but rather a sense of peace. He no longer feared death, and seemed to know that death would come swiftly.

Slowly, Gray Wolf lowered his bow and looked at the intruder. He felt a reluctance to kill this man, although he didn't know why. They looked into each other's eyes and seemed to know the part they were to play. There was no hate between them, simply a role that they had each been destined to fill.

Slowly, Gray Wolf drew back his bow as he raised it to take aim. He hesitated briefly, then let the arrow fly to its mark.

Jacob felt the arrow strike his chest, but he felt no pain. He watched Gray Wolf as he let his bow drop to his side. Jacob knew it was over.

Gray Wolf stood in front of the intruder and watched his enemy die. But, he found it difficult to think of him as his enemy.

As Jacob lay against the boulder, his life slowly slipping away, he whispered, "I'm sorry." Slowly, Jacob's eyes closed and his world turned to darkness. He was dead.

Gray Wolf stood looking at the intruder for several minutes before he simply turned and walked off into the forest followed by his fellow warriors.

STAGE STOP

It would be several hours before the stagecoach was due to arrive at Anton Station, a stage stop on the run from Kansas City to Fort Collins. The station was operated by a widow in her early forties named Martha McCullen and her sixteen-year-old daughter, Jennifer. George Pepper, a stagecoach driver, also helped by bringing supplies from the stage company on his way through.

It was Jennifer's job to have the horses ready to exchange for those that would bring the stagecoach from Cope Corner. After feeding the horses, she pumped water into the horse trough. The horses were trying to stay cool in the shade of the lean-to next to the corral.

When Jennifer finished her chores in the corral, she started back toward the sod house that served as the station. Before entering, she stopped to look out across the vast open space of the prairie. She was impatient for the stagecoach to arrive because Will Simon would be on it.

She first met Will almost a year ago. He was a tall, lean young man who was shy and reserved, but Jennifer quickly found herself thinking about him at all hours and wanting to spend as much time as possible with him. She would talk to him while he hitched up the horses and sit with him while he ate. She dreamed about him almost every night. It was her hope that someday Will would ask her to marry him.

Her thoughts were distracted by the sight of a thin column of dust as it rose in the distance. At first she thought it was a dust devil, but she soon realized it was the stagecoach.

"Mom, the stage is coming," Jennifer called out.

"My land, it's early," Martha said as she stepped out the door to look. "Something's wrong."

"It's just early."

"No, something's wrong. Mr. Pepper would never push a team that hard on a day like this unless there was trouble. Get inside."

Jennifer hesitated for only a second as her thoughts turned to Will. Fear gripped her heart at the thought that he might be hurt, but she did as her mother told her. She stepped inside, but watched to see if she could see Will riding shotgun. She let out a sigh of relief when she saw him sitting next to Mr. Pepper.

Jennifer's mother stepped back inside the station and reached for the rifle that was leaning against the doorframe. She levered a cartridge into the chamber and waited.

The stagecoach's six horses were covered with heavy lather from the hard run. As the stagecoach drew close to the station, George pulled back on the reins, pushed hard on the brake arm with his foot and yelled for the team to stop.

"Whoa! Whoa!"

"What's the matter, George?" Martha asked as she stepped outside.

"We've got an injured passenger aboard."

"Bring him inside," Martha said as she set the rifle down next to the door and went back inside.

George and Will climbed down off the stagecoach, opened the door and lifted the injured man out of the coach. They carried him inside the station and put him on a cot while Martha got a pan of hot water and a few pieces of cloth. The men stepped back out of the way as Martha set the pan on a table next to the bed.

"What happened, George?" Martha asked.

"We come upon some Indians over at Cope Corner, and we had to make a run for it. Wasn't sure we was goin' to get away, but we fought 'um off. Mr. Morris took a bullet while we was gettin' away. We've been pushin' the team pretty hard to get here. Looks pretty bad, don't it?"

"Yes," she replied.

For now, the other passengers would have to wait. Martha went right to work removing Mr. Morris's bloody shirt and washing his wound. Martha didn't notice the woman as she came in, but heard her voice.

"Can I be of some help?"

"I could use an extra hand, if you don't mind."

The woman slipped out of her fancy eastern jacket and rolled up the sleeves of her lacy white blouse.

"What would you want me to do?"

"Help me roll him over, please."

Jennifer gathered up more cloth for bandages and prepared more clean hot water. She watched out of the corner of her eye as the woman knelt down to help her mother.

"I'm Alicia Duncan," the woman said as she looked into Martha's tired eyes.

"I'm Martha McCullen," she replied and quickly returned to caring for Mr. Morris' wound.

George could see that Mr. Morris was in good hands. He turned to the others and directed them outside. Jennifer followed them as far as the door, watching Will as George gave each of the men instructions.

"Will, I want you to unhitch the horses and get 'um in the corral, then go over by those trees and keep an eye out. If'n it moves, I want to know about it."

"Yes, sir," Will replied and ran off toward the coach.

"Mr. Duncan, I need you to help Will with the horses. As soon as you've got 'um in the corral, take the rifle off the coach and keep an eye out from the lean-to."

Duncan looked at George as if he was going to object to being given orders by a stagecoach driver, but he turned and stomped off toward the coach without comment.

"Mr. Sutton, I'd like you to stay near the coach and keep an eye out to the east for anything that ain't normal."

Jennifer stepped aside as George went back inside the station. Alicia and Martha had just finished dressing Mr. Morris' wound and were trying to make him as comfortable as possible.

"How's he doing?" George asked.

"Not very well, I'm afraid," Martha replied just as Mr. Duncan came through the door.

"I think we should hitch up the fresh horses and get out of here while we still can," Duncan blurted out angrily.

"I don't think it would be wise to move Mr. Morris," Martha replied politely.

"I wasn't thinking of taking him. He'd just slow us down. He probably won't live long anyway."

Martha was startled by this man's callousness and didn't know what to say. She looked to Alicia for help, but all she saw was a look of disdain in Alicia's eyes as she stared at her husband.

"You listen to me, Mr. Duncan. I drive the stagecoach and we will go when I say. Right now, we're better off here. There ain't so much as a tree between here and the next station. Now you get back out there and keep your eyes open."

Duncan glanced over at Alicia. When their eyes met, she looked down at the floor as if she was embarrassed that she even knew him. Duncan turned and stormed out the door.

Jennifer stood by the door and listened for a few minutes while George discussed the situation with the two women. The fact that the Indians were on the warpath, reminded her of what had happened to her father only a few years ago when a couple of renegades caught him out hunting alone and killed him.

Jennifer stepped outside and looked around for Will. She felt as if her heart was in her throat when she did not see him right away. The only person she could see was Mr. Duncan, and he was pacing back and forth in front of the corral with a rifle clutched tightly in his hand. He was not watching for Indians, he was too busy pacing and mumbling to himself.

She remembered George had sent Will out to stand guard near the trees around the corner. As she came around the corner, she stopped when she saw Will leaning against a tree. He seemed to be watching something off in the distance.

Will was watching a thin column of smoke rising from a butte off to the north. Will had grown up on the prairie and knew what the smoke meant. Although Will was watching the smoke, he was thinking of Jennifer. He always liked this part of the run best because it gave him a chance to see Jennifer and spend an hour or so near her. The thought of Jennifer being out here with just her mother worried him, especially with the Indians on the warpath.

Will knew he had a job to do for the stage line, and the job was not done until the passengers arrived in Fort Collins safely. He planned to ask Jennifer to marry him as soon as he had a little money saved up, but he was thinking that he might ask her now and take her with him when the stagecoach leaves. He made a silent vow that he would not leave without her.

"What are you thinkin' about, Will?" Jennifer asked softly as she stepped up behind him.

The sound of her voice startled him and he turned in a flash. He caught the sight of her large, soft blue eyes for just a second before he looked down at the ground in front him.

"I was thinkin' about you," he mumbled so quietly that she could hardly hear him.

"Will Simon, I swear you're the shyest man I've ever set eyes on. Now, tell me, what were you thinkin' about?"

"I - - I was thinkin' about you being out here all alone, with no one to protect you."

"I'm not alone," she replied as she stepped up in front of him. "Mom's here, and people stop by now and then."

Without thinking, Will reached out with his free hand and grabbed Jennifer by the arm. "It just ain't safe out here no more. I want you to come with me, and marry me in Fort Collins," he blurted out.

Jennifer could not believe what she had heard. Although the tone of his voice indicated he was angry, his words showed how much he cared for her. He finally admitted he loved her.

"Will, did you just ask me to marry you?"

"Yes, I guess I did," he replied softly.

"Did you mean it?"

"Yes."

"Yes, yes," she replied as she threw her arms around his neck and kissed him.

Will was so surprised and stunned by her reaction that he almost dropped his rifle. The surprise wore off quickly as he felt her young body pressed against him, and the warmth of her lips against his. He had never been kissed like this before, and he liked it.

Jennifer pulled back, looked up at him and smiled. She couldn't remember when she had been so happy, but the feeling was short-lived. Their moment was shattered by the sound of someone yelling, and the thunder of horse's hooves on the dry hard ground. Will pushed Jennifer behind him with his free hand while he readied himself for a fight. Just then Mr. Duncan came charging around the corner on one of the horses, whipping the horse on.

"Stop! Come back!" Will yelled in a feeble effort to get him to return.

With all the noise, George and the two women came running out of the station in time to see Duncan riding off across the prairie. Martha glanced over at Alicia to see her reaction. When Alicia saw Martha looking at her, she simply let out a sigh and looked down at the ground in front of her.

"Maybe, he's going for help," Martha said in an attempt to console Alicia.

"No," she replied softly. "He's looking out for himself. Down deep I knew what he was when I married him, but I'd hoped he would change if he were faced with a real challenge. I never should have insisted that we come west."

Martha couldn't help feeling sorry for Alicia. She reached out and put her arm around Alicia's shoulders and gently guided her back toward the station.

"Damn!" George yelled as he threw his hat on the ground in frustration. "That damn fool just killed himself."

The two women stopped at the door and looked back at the cloud of dust the horse was kicking up as it ran wildly across the prairie.

"You want me to go after him, George," Will ask.

"No. I need you here. I suppose he took one of the fresh horses."

"Yes, sir."

"Damn!" George said again, then turned around. He saw the two women standing only a few yards away.

"Sorry, Ma'am," he apologized, embarrassed that the women might have heard him swear.

"That's all right, George."

"Excuse me, sir. I was wondering what you plan to do now?"

"Well, Mr. Sutton, I don't rightly know. I'll have to think on it some," George replied.

"Do you think it's possible that Mr. Duncan will make it to some place where he can get help for us?"

"I doubt Duncan gave any thought to goin' for help."

George was about to tell Mr. Sutton he didn't think that Duncan stood a snowball's chance in hell of making it to the next stage station, let alone making it to any kind of help. Instead, George decided to hold his tongue and say nothing more.

"Keep your eyes open. We're not out of this yet."

"Yes, sir," Mr. Sutton said as he turned and walked back to the stagecoach.

Will glanced at Jennifer. He took her hand and led her back over to the trees where he could keep watch.

"Jennifer, I want you to go inside with your mother."

"But - -."

"Please."

Jennifer understood. He wanted her inside the station where she would be safe. She wanted to stay with him, but there was much to be done in case the Indians should attack the station. Jennifer rose up on her tiptoes and kissed Will lightly on the cheek. She smiled at him, then turned and walked back to the station.

When Jennifer entered the station, she found George sitting with his elbows on the table and his chin in his hands. She walked to the fireplace where her mother was making coffee.

"What's wrong with Mr. Pepper?"

"Nothing. He's just got a lot on his mind, right now."

"Mom, Will asked me to marry him."

Martha froze as she stared at Jennifer. For a second she didn't know what to say, but she quickly regained her composure.

"And what was your answer?"

"I told him 'yes'," she answered with a big grin.

"Congratulation," Alicia said. "Will seems like a very nice young man, and brave, too."

The joy of the moment came to an abrupt end at the sound of a rifle shot. George stood up and grabbed his rifle from the end of the table as he headed out the door. Martha grabbed the rifle by the door and followed George. Jennifer and Alicia ran to the door to watch from there.

George ran to the stage to find out what Mr. Sutton had seen that was worth shooting at. As he approached the stage, he saw a horse in the distance slowly walking toward them. At first, he wasn't sure if there was a rider on the horse, but as the horse slowly turned they could see a man slumped over the horse's neck.

"Who is it?" Mr. Sutton asked.

"Not sure," George replied as he strained to see who might be out there.

"Is it an Indian?"

"No," he replied as he realized who it was. "It's Duncan."

Sutton looked at George as if he had seen a ghost. If it was Duncan, why wasn't anyone going after him?

"Shouldn't someone go out there and bring him back?"

"No. That's just what the Indians want us to do. Chances are he's already dead."

Just then the body fell off the horse onto the ground.

"What Indians? I haven't seen any Indians. There's no place to hide out there, it's so flat."

"That's where you're wrong. It looks flat, but there are ravines and gullies all over where you could hide a small army. Did you see that horse show up all of a sudden like?"

"Well, yes. It seemed to just pop up out there," Mr. Sutton said as he began to understand what George was telling him.

"My guess would be Duncan was in such a hurry to get away that he rode into a ravine full of Indians. He didn't have a chance. They probably killed him, put him on the horse and sent the horse back out where we could see it."

"You mean it's a trap to get us to come out in the open."

"You catch on right fast, Mr. Sutton."

"What do we do now?"

"We pull the stagecoach as close to the station as we can. Then we wait," George replied.

George gathered everyone together and explained what he wanted to do. The three women and the three men working together were able to move the heavy stagecoach closer to the station on the side nearest the corral.

"Mr. Sutton, I want you on top of the stagecoach. You can see better from up there. Will and I will spell you from time to time."

Mr. Sutton nodded that he understood and climbed up on top of the stagecoach. Alicia handed a rifle and a jug of water up to him. He smiled down at her thinking that he should say something about her husband, but he didn't know what to say.

George didn't know what to say, either. She seemed to be taking her husband's death rather calmly. However, he did notice a small tear rolled down her cheek.

"You all right, Ma'am?"

"Yes. I'll be fine. I know he wasn't a very brave man, but in his own way he wasn't all bad."

"I'm sure he wasn't." George didn't know what else to say, so he excused himself and went looking for Martha.

Martha was standing just outside the door staring out across the prairie. The look on her face was that of a person who had lost someone close. George stopped next to her, put his arm around her shoulders and gazed out over the vast open space. He was sure that the death of Mr. Duncan reminded Martha of the loss of her husband.

"I'm going to miss this place, George."

"Why, where are you going?"

"I don't know, but I can't stay here alone."

"When things settle down, you can come back and pick up where you left off."

"I can't run this place by myself. I won't have Jennifer to help me much longer. Will ask her to marry him."

"I figured. Jennifer was all Will talked about all the way here. But you could run it if you had someone to help, couldn't you?"

"I guess."

"Well, we've known each other for some time and we get along pretty well, wouldn't you say?"

"Yes," she said softly, trying to hold back a smile as she watched George stumble for the right words.

"Well, I've been thinkin' of given up my job driving stagecoaches and findin' me a place to settle down. I was thinkin' this place is kind of nice, and we could run it just fine together."

"What would people say, the two of us out here together?"

"Well, I don't reckon folks would say too much if we was married," George said as he looked down at the ground and pushed some dirt around with the toe his boot.

"Why George, you old coot. How long you been carryin' a torch for me?"

George hesitated to say, but finally admitted after a long pause, "Better 'n three years."

"Would you really want to live out here with me?"

"Ma'am, I'd be right proud to live out here with you. We could get a few head and raise some cows. Maybe, build a barn."

"I guess that settles it. Yes, George, I'll marry you."

George's face turned a little red, but his heart jumped with excitement. He couldn't remember when he had felt so happy about anything, but the sound of another rifle shot quickly brought him back to reality.

"Here they come!" Mr. Sutton yelled.

George pushed Martha back into the station, then ran around the corner of the station. He could hear the sounds of rifle fire coming from on top of the stagecoach, and from where Will had been. Will was pulling back from the trees toward the station. George began firing at the approaching Indians to cover Will's retreat.

Except for Mr. Sutton who was still on the top of the stagecoach, they rushed into the station. Everyone, who was able, grabbed a gun and picked a window to shoot from.

Several of the Indians attempted to get to the horses in the corral, but Will and George concentrated their fire in that direction. After several Indians had been killed or wounded trying to get to the horses, the rest retreated back to a ravine.

As soon as the shooting stopped, everyone took a second to take a breath. Will checked to see if Jennifer was all right, and George glanced over at Martha.

"Well, that took care of that."

Everyone turned toward the door to see Mr. Sutton standing in the doorway with a big grin on his face.

"They'll be back," George said.

"But we beat them."

"They was only testing our strength, and hopin' to get the horses in the process. Since they didn't get the horses, they'll be back," Will said flatly.

"Oh! You've been shot," Alicia cried out.

Everyone looked down at Sutton's left arm and saw blood running down his fingers. In all the excitement, he had not realized that he had been shot. Alicia took him by the arm and guided him to the table. She helped him take off his shirt while Martha got some clean bandages and hot water.

"What do you suggest we do, Mr. Pepper? We can't hold them off forever," Alicia asked as she began cleaning Mr. Sutton's wound.

George wanted to say something that would calm all their fears, but he had no answers. He felt a deep responsibility for everyone here. The station was not an easy place to defend, although, it was better than being out in the open.

Suddenly, there was a bright flash of light immediately followed by the crash of thunder. A quick glance out the window let him know that a sudden summer storm was coming. The wind started to blow, whipping up dust. If the wind blew any harder, it would be hard to see more than a few yards.

George walked over to the window and looked out. With all the dirt and dust blowing around, he could just barely see the horses milling around in the corral. This gave him an idea.

"You women gather up what guns and ammunition you can. Will, cover your face and come with me."

"George, what are you going to do?"

George took hold of Martha's arms as he looked into her frightened eyes.

"We're going to hitch up the stagecoach and get out of here, all of us."

Will was waiting near the door with Jennifer when George turned to leave. Jennifer kissed Will on the cheek, then helped him cover his face with his bandanna. He gave her a wink, then turned and followed George out the door.

The dust and dirt of the prairie whirled around the two men as they struggled to get to the corral. Trying to move against the wind was difficult enough, but not being able to see very far made it worse.

When they finally made it to the corral, they found the horses were nervous and frightened. It was clear the animals would be hard to handle.

"Try 'n get rags over their eyes. It'll make 'um easier to handle," George yelled.

The wind had gotten so strong that his voice didn't carry more than a few feet, but Will managed to hear him enough to understand what he wanted. Will grabbed a burlap bag from inside the lean-to. As soon as George roped a horse, Will covered its eyes with the burlap bag. The horse settled down enough that it could be led to the gate. George tied the horse to the fence, then went after the next one. The two of them worked together until they had six of the horses tied near the gate.

Just as Will was starting to put the harness on one of the horses, a shot rang out from behind. He spun around in time to see an Indian fall to the ground not more than ten feet behind him. He also saw Jennifer standing a little further away with a rifle in her hands. Will ran to her, took her in his arms and led her around the dead Indian to the fence.

"You stay right here and keep your eyes open. We have to get the team hitched up."

Suddenly there was a second shot, then a third, then more. The Indians were using the blowing dirt as cover to get closer. As a shot ran out, one of the horses reared up and fell over backwards, pushing George to the ground as it fell.

Will was too busy trying to keep the Indians from getting to the horses to notice that the horse had fallen on George's leg. With the noise of the wind and the sound of gunfire, it was hard to hear anything else.

A volley of gunfire came from behind Will. He glanced back over his shoulder and saw Alicia, Martha and Sutton rushing to their aid. Jennifer and Martha rushed to help George while Sutton and Alicia joined Will in fighting off the Indians.

Once again, they pushed the Indians back. But like before, not without paying a heavy price. Jennifer and Martha helped George to the station while Will kept watch for another attack. During the lull, they moved six of the horses into the station so the Indians could not get them. The horses were their only hope of getting out, and they needed to protect them.

George's right leg was broken and he was in a great deal of pain. With George laid up, and Sutton limited to the use of one arm, their chances of escaping were growing slim.

There was another flash of light followed by the crash of thunder as they all retreated to the station. It began to rain. The rain came in large drops at first, then quickly turned into a downpour. The rain came too fast for the dry ground to soak it up and the road soon turned into a stream of rushing water.

"What are we going to do now?" Alicia asked. "The road will be too muddy for the horses to pull the stagecoach."

"Go to a window and keep your eyes open," Will ordered. "If you see anything move out there, make sure of your target and shoot."

Martha took a shotgun and stood at the window nearest to the bed George was lying on. She tried to watch outside and keep an eye on him at the same time. She quietly said a prayer that he would be all right.

Jennifer stared out the window that overlooked the corral. She noticed a couple of the horses that had been left in the corral were milling around. At first she thought she was just seeing shadows, but realized someone was in the corral.

"Will, they're in the corral."

Will ran to her side and looked out the window. Patiently, he scanned the lean-to and saw something move. A couple of Indians had gotten into the corral under the cover of the rain and were trying to steal the remaining horses.

"I see them. Let them have the horses. Maybe they will be satisfied and leave," Will said.

Without warning, several shots rang out from the other side of the station with several bullets hitting the building. Will slammed the shutter closed over the window and ducked down. It was clear that the Indians were trying to distract their attention from the corral.

"Close the shutters and keep down," he yelled out. "We don't have a lot of ammunition, so be sure of what you shoot at."

For the next hour or so, rifle shots could be heard as well as the sound of bullets hitting the station. Occasionally, someone from inside the station would shoot back. The horses were restless and not used to being in such confining quarters. Will had tied them to a ceiling beam to keep them from moving around and getting in the way. He left the burlap bags over their eyes in the hope of keeping them calm.

No one felt like talking. This was a time to think, to plan and to pray. Everyone was consumed with their own thoughts. There was little anyone could do for the moment, except keep watch and keep the Indians at bay.

Will looked out a peephole in the heavy wooden shutter. The corral looked empty, the horses were gone. Time passed slowly as they waited and watched. It had been some time since either side had fired any shots.

Jennifer put her hand on Will's shoulder as she sat at his side. There was no need to talk, just being close was enough.

"Will, do you think they've gone?" Alicia asked.

"Don't know. We'll just wait until this storm blows over before we try to find out."

With George laid up, and Sutton injured, the others seemed to look to Will for answers. It was not a job he wanted, but it was sort of forced on him. He had always been shy, but now he had to take charge.

It soon grew dark and the rain slacked off to a slow but steady drizzle. They settled in for a long night, taking turns sleeping and watching. Martha spent most of her time at George's bedside, wiping his brow and making him as comfortable as possible between catnaps.

Alicia checked on Mr. Morris from time to time, made coffee, and made sure that everyone got a little something to eat. When she was not busy looking after the others, she sat close to Mr. Sutton. The two of them spent the long hours talking softly so as not to disturb the others.

Jennifer napped next to Will as he kept a vigil. As the night wore on, Will became sleepy and could hardly keep his eyes open.

Jennifer traded places with him so he could get a little sleep with his head in her lap.

When morning came, Will opened his eyes and looked up at Jennifer. She smiled down at him. Will sat up to look around the room.

Across the room, Mr. Sutton was watching out the peephole while Alicia slept in a chair next to him. Every few minutes Mr. Sutton would look at her to see if she was okay.

George Pepper was lying on a cot looking up at the ceiling. Martha was sitting on the floor next to him with her head resting on his shoulder as she slept.

Mr. Morris was resting quietly on another daybed. Jennifer was not sure if he was sleeping or if he was still unconscious, but he seemed to look better and was breathing normally.

Will stood up and slowly opened one of the shutters, letting the early morning sun shine in. He carefully studied the area around the corral. All the horses that had been left in the corral were gone. He wondered if the Indians had gone, too. His first clue that all was clear was a small herd of five or six antelope grazing a few hundred yards from the corral. Then, he noticed a couple of rabbits hopping around in the grass next to the corral. Will let out a sigh of relief.

"It's over," Will said as he looked around the room.

Shutters began to be opened and the sun was allowed to shine into the station. While the women began to fix breakfast and check on the injured, Will and Mr. Sutton opened the door. Cautiously, they moved outside. Mr. Sutton climbed up on top of the stagecoach to scan the area, while Will walked around the station to see that all was clear.

Once satisfied that there was no longer any danger, Will returned to the station. Will and Jennifer took the horses back to the corral to feed and water them while Mr. Sutton stood guard from on top of the stagecoach.

By noon, the ground was once again dry enough for the stagecoach to be moved. Will hitched up the team while George and Mr. Morris were carefully loaded inside. Once everyone was aboard, Will cracked the whip and the horses started off across the prairie. Will saw the sad look on Jennifer's face as she looked back toward the station.

"We'll be back soon," he assured her.

Jennifer turned and looked at him, then slid close to him. She reached out and rested her hand on his arm. They would be back, but when they returned she would be Mrs. Will Simon.

THE QUEST

The wind was blowing down out of the north. It would not be long before winter would cover the mountains with snow. Winter was coming early to the Black Hills, and Running Elk was wishing that he had gone south with the rest of his tribe. But Running Elk was on a quest, a quest that would take him far away from his friends and family.

Running Elk's beautiful young sister, Wind Song, had been taken by trappers while she was washing clothes in the creek. It had been several hours before anyone realized she was missing. The trappers who took her left almost no trail to follow.

Running Elk did not need a trail to show him the way. He knew where the trappers were taking her. He had heard the stories of beautiful young Indian girls being taken to mining camps where the men there used them.

He rode his pony, and led another, along the narrow trail that would take him down off the ridge into the deep valley below. Once he reached the bottom of the valley, he would have to turn east and follow a small stream until it joined up with Castle Creek. From there, he could follow the creek to Prescott, a small mining town in the central part of the Black Hills.

Running Elk had been riding for six days before he reached the outskirts of Prescott. He had learned from others who had gone into these mining camps before him that they were not a safe place for an Indian. He took care not to be seen as he studied the layout of the town from a ridge above the town. He wondered if his sister was at this mining camp, or if she had been taken somewhere else. No matter, he would find her no matter how long it took.

There were only four buildings in the town that were wooden, the rest were large tents with only wooden fronts. The four buildings were the hotel, two saloons, and a livery stable. Running Elk had never seen a town like this before, although he had heard about them. The street was busy with miners and trappers milling around. A strange looking little man with squinty eyes and a long tail of hair was washing clothes near one of the tents, while women were standing in front of the saloons smoking little brown cigars. It was as if he had entered a different world.

He decided to wait until after dark before trying to find out if his sister was there. As he turned around to return to the woods where he had left his ponies, a voice rang out.

"What the hell you doin'?"

Running Elk saw a short stocky man in tall boots and a heavy buffalo coat step out of the shadows. His face was covered with thick black hair, and his dirty hat was pulled down in front. In his hands, he held a rifle. A quick look around told Running Elk that to run would be unwise.

"I'll bet you come for that new Indian girl at the hotel," the man said in Lakota, the native tongue of the Sioux.

The young warrior was puzzled. The man had spoken in his language, though somewhat crudely.

"You had your tongue cut out?"

"No," Running Elk answered.

"You looking for a young Indian girl?"

"Yes."

"You know where she is?"

"No," he replied reluctantly.

"What's your name?"

"Running Elk."

"I'm called Jonathan Black Wolf. I know your father. He is a great leader and a good man."

"How do you know him?"

"He saved my life once," the half-breed said without further explanation. "Who is this girl to you?"

"She is my sister."

"Your sister!" he said with surprise. "You go into the woods and wait for me. I'll try to find out if she's here. If she is, I'll let her know that you will come for her."

Running Elk was suspicious of this man, but what choice did he have? He would not trust this man, but he would hide in the woods until dark. If this man could find his sister, all the better. But if he couldn't, Running Elk would find her himself.

Black Wolf turned and began walking away. Running Elk looked down for just a second, then back in the direction of Black Wolf. To his surprise, Black Wolf was gone. He had disappeared as quickly and as silently as he had appeared.

Running Elk slipped silently back into the woods to wait for darkness. He found a narrow ledge where he could wait and watch. From his new perch, he could see most of the street.

Suddenly, Running Elk noticed Black Wolf walk up to the front of one of the saloons and stop. Black Wolf briefly talked with two men. While they talked, one of the men turned to look toward where Running Elk had been. After a few minutes, Black Wolf went inside the saloon. The two other men dashed across the street and disappeared between two of the buildings.

Running Elk was sure that Black Wolf had told the men where he could be found. If he waited where he was, they would soon find him. As he started to move, he heard the sounds of someone running through the trees. He was surprised, as he did not think that he would be found so quickly. He stood up and ran off into the deep woods. He could hear the sounds of someone running behind him.

Suddenly, there was a rifle shot and a small branch exploded next to his ear. Running Elk dropped down behind a log, drew an arrow from his quiver, fit it into his bow and drew the string back. As one of the men came dashing out from the trees, he let go of the string. His arrow flew through the air and smashed into the man's chest.

The man stopped and looked down at the arrow sticking out of him. He had a surprised look on his face as he stared at it. He looked up, looking directly at Running Elk for a second or two before he slowly closed his eyes and fell face down on the ground, dead.

The second man ducked down behind a tree, took aim and fired a shot at Running Elk. The bullet whizzed past Running Elk's head. Running Elk quickly dove behind a tree.

Under the cover of the fallen tree and the thick under-growth, Running Elk crawled away. His enemy was not so willing to pursue him into the thick undergrowth now that his friend was dead.

Running Elk made a large circle around the outskirts of the town in an effort to stay out of sight. It took him over an hour to get around to the other side of the town. When he broke out of the woods, he found himself at the back of the hotel. He crouched down among the heavy undergrowth at the edge of the woods to wait for darkness.

Darkness would come early in the late days of October, and it could turn cold fast. Heavy clouds rolled in over the surrounding hilltops and hung over the valley threatening the mining town with the first snow of winter. As darkness came, so did the snow. It started slowly, but gradually became a wet heavy snow that quickly covered the ground. Running Elk did not like to see the snow come for he knew he would leave footprints wherever he went. It would also make his escape with his sister more difficult.

Running Elk waited until the town was quiet before he crawled out of the woods and hid behind a pile of firewood stacked behind the hotel. He ducked down low when the door to the hotel suddenly opened and a man came out. The man gathered an armful of wood, then turned around and went back inside.

Running Elk could see the man's footprints in the light covering of snow. He climbed over the stack of wood and walked in the tracks left by the man. When he reached the door, he opened it. There was a faint glow from a lantern that lit up the small room. Running Elk slipped inside and quietly shut the door. He quickly hid behind a door when he heard voices coming toward him.

"Do you think he will come back?" a man said as he walked into the room.

"He's come to get his sister, what do you think?"

Running Elk immediately recognized the sarcastic voice of the second man. It was Black Wolf.

"What do you suggest we do, since you brought her here?"

"Don't worry. I'll find him, then I'll kill him."

"You better, Wolf. I don't want any trouble. I've already lost one man."

Running Elk watched through the crack in the door as Black Wolf turned on his heels and left the room. The other man took a bottle of whiskey off the shelf, then left, closing the door behind him. Although Running Elk understood very little of the white man's conversation, he understood enough to know that his sister was being held in the hotel, but where?

Running Elk spent the next couple of hours waiting and listening for the hotel to become quiet. It was about two in the morning before Running Elk felt that it had been quiet long enough for everyone to be asleep.

Slowly, he moved across the floor toward the door that would lead him into the main part of the hotel. As he opened the door, he peered out into the lobby. Except for the faint glow of a single lamp, the room was dark and void of anyone.

Carefully, he examined the lobby, looked into the hotel bar and the dining room. Again, they were empty and quiet. He looked up the stairs. Running Elk drew his knife and started up the stairs. He stopped suddenly when he put his foot down on a step that squeaked. He held his breath as he waited and listened to see if anyone had heard it. When he heard no other sounds, he once again moved up the stairs.

He stopped at the top of the stairs and looked down the hall. In the dim glow of a night-light, he could see seven doors, three on each side of the long hall and one at the end. There was no one standing guard at any of them. There was only one thing he could do. He would have to check behind each door if he was going to find his sister.

He silently moved down the hall to the first door. After listening at the door and hearing nothing, he carefully reached for the doorknob and slowly turned it. The door opened. He pushed it open far enough to see in, but he could see nothing. Suddenly, he was startled by a harsh voice.

"This room's taken. Get lost."

He quickly closed the door and leaned against the wall. He held his knife tightly in his hand, not sure if he was going to have to use it. When it remained quiet, he moved across the hall to the next door. Again, he carefully opened the door and peeked in. In the darkness he could see nothing, but he could hear the deep raspy sounds of a man snoring. Quietly, he closed the door.

The next two rooms were also occupied by snoring men, probably sleeping off an evening of drinking at one of the saloons. When he got to the fifth door, he could see light at the bottom of the door. There was no doubt that there was someone in the room and that they were still up.

Running Elk moved up to the door, leaned against it and listened. He could hear the sound of a man talking, but could not understand what he was saying. He was about to go on to the last door when he thought that he heard something said in his native tongue. He stopped to listen again.

Suddenly, he was interrupted by the sound of someone coming up the stairs. He looked around for some place to hide, but saw nothing. He started for the door at the end of the hall, but was spotted before he could get out.

"In'jun," the man yelled.

Just as Running Elk dashed out the door, a shot rang out and a bullet smashed into the doorframe. Running Elk disappeared out the door, slamming the door shut before another shot could be fired.

"What's going on out here, Wilber?"

"There was an in'jun outside your door, Mr. Roth. He had a big knife in his hand."

Roth looked toward the back door of the hotel. Black Wolf had not taken care of the Indian after all. By this time several of the hotel guests were looking out their doors to see what all the commotion was about.

"Everything is fine. We just had someone here that didn't belong, but he's gone now. You can all go back to sleep."

Roth motioned for the guests to go back to bed. He watched down the hall until he was sure that everyone had returned to their rooms, then grabbed Wilber by the arm.

"I want you to find Black Wolf and tell him to get up here, now. And find the others, I want that Indian found."

"Yes, sir."

Roth watched Wilber as he hurried down the hall. As soon as he was out of sight, Roth took another look up and down the hall before stepping back into his room and closing the door.

Roth leaned back against the door as he tried to think. He looked over at the Indian girl who was tied and laying on the bed. She was very beautiful, but he was wondering if he had made a big mistake by buying this girl from the trappers. He had bought girls from trappers before, but this one might turn out to be more trouble than he had planned on.

As he looked at the girl, he noticed something different about her. She had been a very frightened girl earlier, but the look in her eyes was more defiant now. Did she know that someone was coming to get her? Did she know who the Indian in the hall was?

"What is it you know, that I should know? I wish I could speak your language," Roth said as he looked at the girl.

Running Elk had made his escape by climbing up on the handrail of the outside stairs and onto the roof. He lay flat on the roof while others were running around on the ground looking for some sign of where he went. With all the commotion below him, he knew that it would not be long and there would be so many tracks on the ground that no one would be able to tell if his were among them, or not.

The heavy wet snow continued to fall. Running Elk grew cold and wet lying on the roof while he waited for everyone to settle down and go back to sleep. Once it was quiet again, he slid off the roof onto the railing. He dropped down on the landing, looked around and tried to open the door. It was locked. He drew his long sharp hunting knife and quickly pried opened the door. After a quick look around, he stepped inside the hallway, closing the door behind him.

Running Elk quickly and quietly moved down the hall to the door where he had heard a girl speak his language. Although the sound of the voice was not clear, he was sure that it was his sister. Without further delay, Running Elk slammed his body against the door. The door instantly gave way, and he found himself crashing through the door and ending up face down on the floor in the middle of the room.

Roth was standing by the bed and quickly turned to see what was happening. Seeing Running Elk on the floor, he grabbed his gun and the girl.

"You are very persistent," Roth said as Running Elk looked up at him.

Slowly, Running Elk stood up. He looked at Roth with hatred in his eyes. He would have gladly killed Roth except for the fact that he had a gun to his sister's head.

"Are you all right?" Running Elk asked Wind Song in their native language.

"Yes, now that you are here," she replied.

"Cut the chatter," Roth said as he slowly turned the gun from Wind Song's head and pointed it at Running Elk.

"You are a dead in'jun," Roth said as he pulled the hammer of the gun back.

Just as the hammer fell against a cartridge, Wind Song kicked Roth, spoiling his aim. The bullet slammed into the wall just over Running Elk's shoulder. Running Elk lunged at Roth and wrestled him to the floor. The two men rolled around on the floor as Roth tried to get a shot at Running Elk, and Running Elk tried to stab Roth. Roth had gained the upper hand and was getting Running Elk pinned to the floor when suddenly a heavy water pitcher shattered and Roth collapsed on top of Running Elk.

Running Elk rolled Roth off him and looked up to see his sister standing with the remains of water pitcher in her hand. Running Elk scrambled to his feet and grabbed Wind Song by the arm. He turned toward the door and started to pull her along, but stopped suddenly, pushing Wind Song behind him. Black Wolf had suddenly appeared in the door, rifle in hand. Running Elk slowly backed away as he prepared to fight.

Black Wolf glanced from Running Elk to Roth who was still unconscious on the floor. "I see that you got the best of Roth," Black Wolf said in Lakota.

"He is not dead," Running Elk replied.

"He looks dead to me. You're in a great deal of trouble. I'll help you, but you must do as I say."

"Why should I trust you?"

"You shouldn't, but I owe your father for my life. Tonight I will repay him by letting you go. Go out the back door and don't stop to look around. I will not be able to keep them from coming after you for very long."

Running Elk quickly decided that it was his only chance to get his sister away from here. He started toward the door. Black Wolf stepped aside to let them pass. As they stepped out into the hall, Black Wolf followed them, and watched as they went out the back door and down the stairs.

Just before turning the corner of a building, Running Elk looked up at the back door of the hotel in time to see Black Wolf give him a slight nod, then duck back inside. They worked their way along the back of several buildings and tents, then ducked back into the woods.

Running Elk and Wind Song had not been prepared for the sudden change in the weather. If they did not find some blankets or a place where they could get out of the cold, their escape would be for nothing. In the flimsy clothes her captures had dressed her in, Wind Song would get sick, or freeze to death in a very short time. He had no choice but to return to the town.

"We have to go back".

"We can't," she objected. "I would rather die than go back."

"You will die if we don't find a warm dry place to hold up until I can get warmer clothes," he said.

"We will sneak back into town. We can hide in the livery stable. It will be warm there. I will find you something warm to wear until we join our people."

Wind Song reluctantly gave in. She knew he was right, but going back to that dreadful town frightened her.

They worked their way around to a place behind the livery stable. Wind Song waited in the trees near the corral while Running Elk made sure it was safe. Running Elk found a wide board on the back of the stable that was loose. He pulled on it a couple of times before it moved far enough that he could slide in behind it and get into the stable. Once inside, he looked around to make sure it was safe. No one was around at this late hour.

Running Elk returned for his sister. She followed him into the stable. He found an old blanket lying in the corner, picked it up and motioned for Wind Song to go up into the loft where he wrapped her in the blanket. He led her around to the back of the hay pile and covered her with hay to keep her warm and safe.

"I will be back soon. Don't make any noise," he instructed her.

Running Elk left the loft. He had no idea where he would find clothes that would keep Wind Song warm. He opened the door to the stable and looked out. The snow had stopped, but it was still very cold and damp. There was a slight tint of light in the gray sky. It would not be long before the owner of livery stable would be coming to care for his horses, and open for business.

Running Elk came up with an idea when he saw the strange little man with the pigtail and squinty eyes carrying a basket of clothes. He watched the man as he went into a tent. Running Elk wondered what this man was doing. Where did he get all the clothes? It was then that he noticed the clothes hanging on ropes behind the tent. He was sure that the man was washing clothes, but he had never heard of a man doing woman's work.

Running Elk slipped out of the stable and looked down the street. The street was empty, but he knew it would not be long before the town would wake up. He ran across the street and ducked down alongside the tent the little man had gone in. He waited and listened. He could hear strange music coming from inside.

Running Elk crept around to the back of tent and peered in. The little man had his back to him and did not see Running Elk. A quick glance around the tent showed rows and rows of clothes drying on ropes strung across the tent. The little man was singing as he scrubbed clothes in a large tub of soapy water.

Running Elk snuck into the tent. Quietly and carefully, he picked out pants, shirts and jackets for himself and Wind Song. He slipped back out of the tent as quietly as he had entered. He hurried across the street to the stable and climbed up into the loft.

Wind Song and Running Elk quickly dressed in the white man's clothes. They were not very comfortable and did not fit well, yet they provided warmth. The warmth they needed if they were going to travel in this weather.

Running Elk led Wind Song down from the loft. They were able to sneak out the back of the stable only seconds before the owner came in the front. Running along the corral, they quickly moved into the woods. As soon as they got to where Running Elk had hidden his ponies, he lifted Wind Song up on one of the ponies. As he reached for the reins, he heard the snapping of a twig behind him. Running Elk slowly turned around and saw Black Wolf standing only fifteen feet away, watching them. Black Wolf had his rifle cradled in his arms as he leaned against a tree. Black Wolf had already saved Running Elk's life once, he was not sure that Black Wolf would do it again.

"You know that I should kill you right now, but I won't," Black Wolf said. "Go south for about a mile, you'll find a trail that leads into a canyon. Near the end of the canyon you will come to a stream. Follow that stream and it will take you to the Cheyenne River. You should be safe, and you will have good protection from the weather. Keep moving south and west, you should join your people in a few days."

"Will you come along? I know my father......."

"No. Someone has to lead Roth and his men away. You know he will come after you?"

Running Elk did not understand this man. He wasn't even sure if he should trust him, yet he had helped them escape earlier.

Black Wolf noticed that Running Elk seemed to be hesitant to leave. "You must go and go now. Tell your father about me," he insisted.

Running Elk nodded, then mounted his pony and glanced toward Black Wolf before turning his pony south. Wind Song quickly fell in behind. At first, they rode at an easy gallop that covers ground quickly, but doesn't wear on the ponies as much as running.

They hadn't gone very far when they heard the sound of gun shots. Running Elk reined up and looked back toward Prescott. Several more shots were fired. They seemed to be coming from the other side of the town. He was sure that Black Wolf had done what he said he would do.

Running Elk turned and led Wind Song on south. In the next three days, they saw no one following them. On the fourth day, they were able to join up with the rest of their tribe. When Running Elk told his father about Black Wolf and what he had done, Running Elk's father simply said, "He kept his word."

"What was his word?" Running Elk asked. "And who is he?"

"Black Wolf is my brother's son. I saved his life once, many years ago. He promised that some day he would return the favor."

THE BOUNTY HUNTER

It was a cold, rainy evening when a lone rider rode into the small prairie town of Wild Horse in the Colorado Territory. As the rain ran off the brim of his hat and down his slicker, he stopped in front of the saloon. His horse shook the water from its mane, then stood motionless as the rider looked around.

Wild Horse was not much of a town. A bank, a mercantile store, a hotel, a livery stable and a saloon made up the businesses. The rider turned his horse and nudged him along the muddy street toward the stable.

A man stood in the door of the stable watching it rain. His attention was drawn to the rider moving slowly toward him. He motioned for the rider to come in out of the rain. Once inside the stable, the rider stepped out of the saddle and untied his saddlebags.

"Nasty night, hey?" the stable owner said.

The rider turned and looked at the stable owner. There was something about this rider that made a man's blood turn cold. He was tall, with broad shoulders. His features were hard and his skin was like leather from years out in the open. His thick black mustache was peppered with gray and sat below a nose that had been broken several times. His steel gray eyes were cold and penetrating. The stable owner instantly knew that he was a man of few words, and not a man to anger.

"That'll be two bits a night, mister. That includes a rub down and a servin' of oats with his hay."

As the rider pushed his slicker aside and reached into his pocket for the money, the handgrip of a well-used pistol was revealed. He gave the stable owner the two bits, then drew his rifle from the scabbard. He tucked the rifle under his arm and walked out into the rain without a word. The stable owner watched the man as he walked toward the hotel.

The town marshal was also watching the stranger from his office window. Years of being a lawman told him that this stranger was a dangerous man. As the stranger passed by a lighted window, the marshal thought he recognized him. If he was right, the stranger was Samuel Bolt, a bounty hunter.

Marshal Stone wondered what brought a man like him to his town. Something deep down inside told him that Bolt was not just passing through, he had come here with a purpose.

Sam Bolt walked into the hotel and laid his saddlebags and rifle on the counter. The clerk looked at him, then stepped up to the counter.

"I want a room in front," Sam said as if he expected his request to be honored without question.

"Yes, sir," the clerk replied as he turned the register around and handed Sam a pen.

Sam scribbled his name, then laid the pen on the counter. He held out his hand for a key.

"Second door on the right, Mr. Bolt," the clerk said as he gave Sam the key.

The clerk watched as Sam went up the stairs. Sam had no more then disappeared around the corner, when Marshal Stone came in. The clerk looked at the marshal, then toward the stairs.

"Was that Sam Bolt?"

"Yes. Is he after somebody, Marshal?"

"Not that I know of. What room?"

"Second on the right."

Marshal Stone nodded, then started up the stairs. When he arrived at the door to Bolt's room, he knocked.

"Who is it?" Sam asked as he drew his gun and moved cautiously toward the door.

"Marshal Stone."

Sam opened the door. When he saw Marshal Stone, he holstered his gun and motioned for the marshal to come in.

"What can I do for you, Marshal?"

"You can tell me what you're doin' here."

"I come to get a man that's wanted over in Springfield."

"Who yah after?"

"Billy Garvey."

"You got any idea what you're in for? The Garveys own half of this county. What's he done?"

"He got drunk and got himself into a gunfight. He killed a young farm boy. A saloon girl got killed during the gunfight."

"That happens when bullets start flyin'. Was it a fair fight?"

"If you think killin' a fourteen year old farm boy is a fair fight, I guess it was fair. There's a reward for him. He has to stand trial," Sam said as he pulled a reward poster out of his shirt pocket and handed it to the marshal.

Marshal Stone unfolded the poster and looked at it. It was real, all right. There was a reward of two hundred dollars for Billy Garvey alive, or one hundred dollars for him dead.

"What's your interest in this? I've never heard of you goin' after anyone for less 'n five hundred dollars."

"The dance hall girl was a friend of mine. Besides, I don't like bullies that force a boy into a fight. The kid didn't even have a gun. They had to stick one in his belt. He tried to walk away, but Garvey wouldn't let it be."

"This may turn out to be the hardest hundred dollars you've ever tried to collect," Stone said as he handed the poster back.

"Just don't cause me no problems," Stone added, then turned and walked out of the room.

Sam looked at the door as he stuffed the poster back into his pocket. He thought about what Marshal Stone had said. He was sure that Stone was probably right. This very well could be the toughest job he'd ever taken on.

Sam went to the window and looked out over the street. The rain had let up, but there was still a light drizzle. He watched Marshal Stone cross the street and return to his office. His attention quickly turned to four men who rode into town and stopped in front of the saloon.

The men dismounted, tied their horses to the hitching rail and stepped up on the covered walkway. One of the men removed his hat and slapped it against his leg to shake the water off. Sam instantly recognized him as Billy Garvey.

He watched as the men went into the saloon. As soon as they were out of sight, he looked around. It was dark and the street was empty. This would be as good a time as any to arrest Billy.

Sam grabbed his hat off the bedpost and walked down the stairs to the lobby. He stopped in the lobby and turned toward the desk clerk.

"Give me that scattergun you keep under the counter," Sam demanded of the clerk.

The clerk hesitated, but only for a second before handing over the shotgun. Sam checked the gun, then left the hotel. He walked across the street to the saloon. After stepping up on the walkway, he leaned up against the building between the door and one of the windows.

Peering into the saloon, Sam saw only seven people. There was the bartender, a dance hall girl, the four that just rode in, and a man in a black hat and coat sitting at a table at the back of the room.

Sam watched as Billy Garvey picked up his beer and walked over to the table. He talked for a minute or so with the man in the black hat, then sat down while the others remained at the bar.

Sam pulled back and leaned up against the wall to think. He knew he was outnumbered, but that was not his only problem. With his pistol in one hand and the shotgun in the other, he had no doubt that he could take Billy right here. The question that kept haunting him was would the man in the black hat deal himself into this, or would he stay out of it? If he did deal himself in, whose side would he be on?

Sam knew there was only one way to find out. He tucked the shotgun under his arm while he checked his pistol. When he was ready, he took his pistol in one hand and the shotgun in the other. He quickly stepped through the door and to the side, putting the wall at his back.

"Don't nobody move less'n you plan to die tonight," Sam bellowed.

Two of the three men at the bar thought about doing something brave, but looking down the barrel of that scattergun Sam had pointed in their direction quickly changed their minds. The man in the black hat very carefully laid his cards down and put his hands flat on the table. The dance hall girl stood at the end of the bar with the bartender, neither of them making a move.

"Billy Garvey," Sam called out.

Billy slowly turned around and looked at Sam. He took his time looking Sam over. He did not recognize this man wheeling a shotgun and a pistol.

"What do you want old man?" Billy said.

"I'm takin' you back to Springfield to stand trial for the death of Melody Sparks."

"Who the hell is she?"

"She was the dance hall girl you killed when you murdered that farm boy."

"You callin' me a murderer?"

"I'm callin' you what you are. Now, you comin' back with me peaceable like, or hung over the back of a horse?"

"I'm not going anywhere with you."

"You get up and walk slowly toward me, or I'll kill yah right where you sit."

Suddenly, there was the sound of glass breaking. Sam's attention was distracted for a split second before he dove for the floor. He swung his shotgun around and sent a blast of buckshot through the window just as a shot rang out and a bullet smashed into his leg.

Sam quickly turned back in time to see Billy with a gun in his hand ready to take a second shot, but another blast from the scattergun cut him down before he could pull the trigger. At almost the same time, two pistol shots were fired and two of the men at the bar fell to the floor.

Sam had only fired one shot toward the men at the bar. He glanced toward the man in the black hat and saw him holding a gun. It was pointed at the one remaining man at the bar, and he had his hands up. He wanted no part of this fight.

The fight had lasted only a few seconds, but the room was filled with the smell of burnt gunpowder and the cries of a man in pain. Billy Garvey and one of his men were dead. Another was gut shot and would die before this night was over.

Sam took a deep breath and tried to relax. His leg felt like it was on fire. As he sat up and leaned against the wall, the dance hall girl came over to him carrying a towel. She looked down at him for a moment, then bent down and wrapped the towel tightly around his leg.

As she wrapped his wound, she glanced up at him. He was not a handsome man, but his eyes revealed a man who could be kind and gentle when he wanted or needed to be.

"Thanks, Ma'am," Sam said softly as he gritted his teeth from the pain.

"Jenny," she replied with a smile.

"Thanks, Jenny," he said softly as he looked at her face.

Just then Marshal Stone came running into the salon. He saw the three men on the floor, and Jenny leaning over Sam.

"We better get you some place safe. When old man Garvey finds out you killed his only son, he'll be coming after you."

As Stone helped Sam to his feet, Sam looked over at the man in the black hat. The man stood up and walked toward him.

"I'm mighty obliged for your help, mister," Sam said.

"No problem. I didn't like that little snake anyway."

"Mind if I ask what your name is?"

"Wickem, George Wickem."

"Thanks again, Mr. Wickem."

Stone and Jenny helped Sam out of the salon and across the street to his room.

"Well, you got your man. Now you better hightail it out of here 'fore his old man gets wind of what you've done."

"He can't ride with this leg, Marshal. It needs to be cared for," Jenny said as she leaned over his leg to check his wound.

"I can't protect him here, not from old man Garvey."

"I'll hide him at my place until he can ride," Jenny said.

"I can't let you do that, people will talk," Sam cautioned her.

Jenny smiled, "People already talk."

"Say, Stone. Who's that Wickem fellah? I ain't never heard of him."

"He's a gambler, and a bit of a gunfighter, I'm told."

"I wonder why he dealt himself into this?"

"Don't know."

Sam was thinking about what Stone had said as Jenny and Stone helped him to his feet. It didn't make sense.

"We better take him out the back way. We don't want anyone seeing where we're taking him," Stone said.

With Stone on one side of him and Jenny on the other, they helped him down the back stairs of the hotel to the alley. Working their way along the alley, they soon came to a small cabin. Jenny opened the door and helped Sam inside. After they laid Sam on the bed, Stone looked down at him.

"I don't know how long we can keep this a secret. Old man Garvey is bound to find out where you're hiding."

"Stone, did you see who broke the window in the saloon just before the shootin' started?"

"No."

Sam was looking into Stone's eyes. He couldn't be sure, but something told him that Stone was lying. It made him wonder if Stone had broken the window. Why would Stone break the window? He thought he noticed that Stone was getting a little fidgety, like maybe he had something to hide.

"I got to be goin'," Stone said suddenly.

"Thanks again," Sam said as he watched Stone leave.

After Jenny had helped Sam out of his pants, she cleaned and dressed his leg wound. When she was finished, she covered him with a blanket.

"I got to go," Jenny said. "If I don't get back soon, they might figure out that I was helpin' you a little more than I should. You goin' to be all right?"

"I'll be fine if you hand me that gun over there. I thank yah kindly, but I don't think you should be takin' a risk like this for me."

"I'll be fine," she said with a smile as she handed Sam his gun.

Sam laid his gun across his chest as he watched Jenny leave. His thoughts turned to Marshal Stone. If he had provoked the gunfight by breaking the window, what reason did he have? If he didn't, then who did?

Sam's leg burned and ached something terrible, but he lay still and listened to the sounds of the night. He knew it would not be long before old man Garvey would know what had happened to his son.

Sam was tired and found himself dozing off and on through the night. At one point, he woke and noticed that it was starting to get light outside. He could see around the room a little. He noticed that Jenny had come in sometime during the night and was sleeping in a chair across the room from him. He chose not to disturb her and dozed off.

When he woke again, he could see Jenny in the kitchen at the wood stove fixing breakfast. He watched her as she turned the strips of bacon in the iron frying pan.

"Good mornin'," he said.

"Good mornin'. How are you feelin' this mornin'?" she asked as she looked over her shoulder at him.

"Better. I don't think I should stay here. Garvey will be lookin' for me. If you're hidin' me, he might make it pretty hard on you."

"What am I supposed to do, throw you out in the street?" she asked with a smile.

"I certainly hope not."

"Well then, that's settled. Breakfast is about ready."

Jenny finished fixing breakfast and served it to Sam in bed. Sam ate in silence, his mind was going fast in an effort to think of what he should do. He knew he should not be here, but where could he go? He also knew that Jenny's life would not be pleasant since she had helped him. He came up with an idea.

"Jenny, would you be interested in movin' away from here?"

"And just where would I go?"

"Springfield," he answered as he watched her for a reaction.

Jenny knew Sam was from Springfield. But what was he really asking of her? She knew that she would not be safe here in Wild Horse once old man Garvey found out she had provided Sam with a place to hide, and had cared for his wound.

"My friend, the one Billy killed, left all her things to me. If you were to come back to Springfield with me, you could have them. I'm sure you could wear her clothes, you're about the same size."

"Why, Sam Bolt, you're askin' me to take her place."

"No," he said softly. "I'm offerin' you a safer place to live."

"No you're not. You want from me what you had with Melody. You want me to take her place in your life."

"No," he insisted. "I admit I wouldn't mind, but that's something we'd have to wait and see about after we get to know each other better. You're a right smart lookin' woman and you got a lot of crust, but only time will tell if you and I could have what Melody and I had."

Jenny thought about what he was saying. It was clear to her that Sam and Melody had had something very special. She wondered if they could have that same something special. There was no doubt about what her life would be like around here, but there was a lot of doubt about what her life would be like if she went to Springfield with him.

Jenny's thoughts were suddenly interrupted by a knock on the door. She looked from the door to Sam. Her eyes quickly moved to his gun as she heard him cock the hammer back.

"It's me, Marshal Stone."

Sam nodded for Jenny to let him in. As she walked toward the door, Sam slipped his gun under the covers. Jenny looked back to make sure Sam was ready before opening the door.

"Mornin' Marshal," Jenny said as she stepped back.

"Mornin' Jenny. How's Sam doin'?"

"I'm doin' just fine," Sam replied from the bedroom.

"I sure hope you are 'cause Will Garvey's on his way into town to kill you," he said as he stood in the doorway to the bedroom.

"How long 'fore he'll get here?"

"Maybe a couple of hours. What yah gonna do?"

"I sure as hell can't run, and I can't stay here. How 'bout helpin' me over to the saloon?"

"You can't be runnin' around on that leg. It'll start bleedin' again," Jenny protested.

Sam could see the concerned look on her face and in her eyes.

"I don't have much choice. I can't fight him here."

"You could leave here in a wagon. I'd go with you."

Sam looked at her as he suddenly realized what she was saying. But he also knew what would happen if they left and Will Garvey caught up with them out on the prairie.

"I can't leave now. Garvey will dog my heels until he finds me. We'll have no peace until this is settled once and for all."

"You men are all alike. Well, I'm not waitin' around to see you get killed," Jenny said, then stormed out the door.

Sam didn't know what to say. He looked from the door to Marshal Stone. Stone stood there and looked at Sam.

"Don't just stand there, help me get dressed."

After Sam was dressed, Stone helped him to the saloon. Sam looked at a table in a back corner. From there he could see anyone coming into the saloon before they had a chance to see him. It also put him in the darkest corner. Anyone coming in would be unable to see him for a few seconds while their eyes adjusted to the change in light.

"This'll be fine," Sam said as he laid his pistol and shotgun on the table and settled into the chair.

"You all set, Sam?"

"Yeah, except for a cup of coffee."

"I'll have the bartender get you one. I'd best be getting' back to my office."

Sam's leg still hurt, but he felt safer here where he could see what was going on. As he sipped at the hot black coffee and waited, he wondered about Stone. He was convinced that Stone was a good man, but he would not be the first good man who yielded under the pressures of a powerful man like Will Garvey.

Sam's thoughts turned to Jenny. He wondered where she was at this moment.

"Barkeep, where's Jenny?"

"Don't know, Mr. Bolt. She usually goes for a ride in the mornin'."

Sam nodded his head as if he understood. He wondered if that was what she was doing. If it was, she was a smart girl not to change her normal routine. It distanced her from him. He couldn't help but think the further people stayed away from him, the safer they would be.

Sam's thoughts were interrupted by the sound of several horses moving along the street out in front. Staying alert, he looked out the front door as he watched four or five riders move slowly passed the front of the saloon. He had never met Will Garvey, but he was sure he would know him when he saw him.

He could see a couple of the riders through the front window. They tied their horses in front of the hotel and went inside. He was sure they were checking to see if he was in the hotel. He waited, knowing full well it would be just a matter of minutes before they would be coming after him in the saloon.

"Sam Bolt," a husky voice called out from the street. "We know you're in there. You best come out."

"If you want to talk to me, you'll have to come in here," Sam yelled back as he closed his fingers around his pistol.

"You killed my son. If I have to come in after you, you'll regret it."

"He didn't have to die. If he'd come peaceable, he'd still be alive."

"You had no right to come after him."

"There was a reward out for him in Baca County."

"This ain't Baca County, this is Cheyenne County. You got no authority here."

Sam knew this conversation was going nowhere. He was sure that it was a decoy so some of Garvey's men could get into position. The more they talked, the more time Garvey had to get ready. Sam also knew he didn't have much choice. He could not move very fast with a bum leg.

"Barkeep, I think you better hightail it out of here 'fore you get caught in the middle."

"Mr. Bolt, Billy Garvey needed killin'. He's had the marshal in a corner for some time now."

"Did the marshal break that window last night?"

"Yeah. He was hoping to provoke a gunfight so that either you or Wickem could kill Billy. The marshal isn't fast enough to do it himself."

"Thanks. You better go."

The barkeep nodded that he understood and started out from behind the bar. He stopped suddenly, reached under the bar and pulled out another shotgun. He took it and laid it on the table in front of Sam.

"This might help some," he said, then walked out of the saloon with his hands up.

"You're all alone now, Bolt. Don't you think it's time to come out?"

Sam pushed the heavy table over and slid off his chair onto the floor. He checked his weapons and put them in easy reach. It was only a matter of time before Garvey would lose patience and send his men in after him.

Sam didn't have time to think about his leg, but the burning pain reminded him. He lay on the floor, his back in the corner, as he waited and listened for any sounds that might give him some idea of what was going on outside. It was almost too quiet.

Suddenly, Sam heard the sound of a board creak just to the left of the window. Sam raised his pistol and pointed it toward the window. Just as a pistol barrel came into view, Sam pulled the trigger and shot a hole through the wall just to the left of the window. There was a loud cry of pain and the sound of a gun falling on the floor.

Almost immediately, shots began to ring out. Bottles above the bar began breaking, mirrors shattered and the glass globes on the kerosene lamps crashed to the floor. Bullets flew around the room splintering woodwork and punching holes in the walls.

Sam laid low in the corner, hoping a stray bullet wouldn't hit him. He held onto his guns tightly. He was ready, ready for anyone who might decide to rush in when the shooting stopped.

The rain of bullets stopped as abruptly as it had begun. His palms were wet and clammy, and sweat rolled down his face. He was outnumbered and he knew it. He knew that his chances of surviving this day were slim to none. If he were a betting man, he would not take a bet on his chances of being alive at sunset.

"You still alive in there," Will Garvey said with a slight laugh in his voice.

It was clear he thought that Sam, if not dead, would be pretty badly shot up and ready to give up. Sam didn't answer. Instead, he kept his eyes moving and his ears open to any noise that might give him a clue as to where his enemy might come from next.

There was a long silence, and Sam's mouth was feeling dry. His attention was drawn to the almost inaudible sound of a door opening. If someone was coming in through the back door, he would be only a few feet away when he came around the corner. Sam concentrated on the corner and pointed the shotgun in that direction, but he also kept an eye toward the front door.

Suddenly, all hell broke loose. A man rushed through the front door at the same time another jumped through the broken front window. A third man rushed around the corner firing his gun in the general direction of Sam.

One blast of Sam's scattergun took out the man who rushed in from the back. A second blast hit the man rushing in the front door. A couple of quick shots from Sam's pistol at the man who had come through the window forced him to take cover behind the bar.

Sam dropped the empty shotgun and grabbed up the one the barkeep had given him. Sam fired again at the wounded man as he tried to scramble for cover behind the table he dumped over. A couple more shots into the bar kept the man who dove behind it pinned down.

There was a lull in the fighting that gave Sam a chance to reload the one shotgun and to ready himself. It was not over, he knew that. It would not be over until he was dead, or until Will Garvey was dead.

Sam took a deep breath. He could hear the movement behind the bar, but could not tell where the man was. He listened and watched, occasionally glancing over at the wounded man behind the table.

Suddenly, a shot rang out and a bullet tore through Sam's arm causing him to drop his pistol. As the pain of another wound gripped him, the shotgun went off scattering buckshot into the front of the bar. Before he knew what was happening, someone kicked the shotgun from his hand while someone else kicked him several times, at least once in the head. He was dazed by the kick to the head.

Barely conscious, he could feel himself being lifted up by the arms, then dragged out of the saloon into the street. The bright morning sunlight blinded him. His body was racked with pain, and his head was spinning.

As his head cleared a little and his eyes adjusted to the sunlight, he could see Will Garvey standing only a few feet in front of him. At first, he didn't know how he was able to stand. As his clouded mind began to grasp the situation, he realized that he was being held up by two of Garvey's men.

"Give him a gun," Garvey ordered.

Sam watched as one of Garvey's men put a gun in his empty holster. The two men let go of him and backed away. Sam almost fell, but managed to keep his balance although he was not very steady.

"You killed my son, now you are going to pay."

"Your son was a cold blooded murderer. He deserved to die."

Sam knew he didn't have a chance. His arm hung limp at his side. He would not be able to draw and shoot no matter how hard he tried. He knew that today was his day to die, and he was prepared. He watched as Garvey went for his gun.

Suddenly, shots began to ring out from all directions. Sam was surprised to see several bullets rip through Garvey's body. As Garvey fell to the ground dead, Sam looked around. All of Garvey's men stood flat-footed, totally surprised by the suddenness of the shots from all different directions. Those with guns in their hands simply dropped them. The others stood silently, wondering what was happening.

Marshal Stone stepped out of the hotel onto the front porch with a rifle in his hands. Then George Wickem stepped out of the mercantile store with his fancy pistols in his hands. Other town folks started coming out of buildings, armed and ready to fight for what was theirs.

As Sam watched, Garvey's men were looking at all the armed citizens coming toward them. They put their hands in the air.

Sam was too amazed at what was happening to hear the soft footsteps of someone coming up behind him. Just as he started to lose his balance, he felt someone grab him and support him. He turned and looked to see Jenny at his side, holding him.

George Wickem walked up beside him and helped Jenny hold him. As they began to help him off the street, he stopped and looked over at Marshal Stone.

"You broke the window in the Saloon last night, didn't you?"

"Yes."

"Why? Didn't you know that it would cause a gunfight?"

"Yes, I knew it would. I couldn't take on Garvey alone. You and Wickem, together offered me the best chance to rid this town of him. He has been runnin' this town for years, and anyone who tried to stop him ended up dead."

"Stone hired me to get rid of Garvey and his men, but you showed up before I could do the job," Wickem said.

Sam looked at Jenny. She was looking up at him.

"Come on. Let's get you out of here," she said softly.

Wickem and Jenny helped Sam to Jenny's cabin. Once he was in her bed, she cleaned and dressed his wounds. She made him as comfortable as possible, then sat down in a chair beside the bed.

Sam turned his head and looked at this woman who had twice taken care of him. She was a very special woman, much like Melody had been.

"You get some rest," Jenny said. "When you feel up to it, we'll go to Springfield."

Jenny stood up, leaned down and kissed him lightly on the forehead. She smiled down at him before she left the room so he could rest. Sam closed his eyes and drifted off to sleep with a slight smile on his face.

THE DEADWOOD
STAGECOACH ROBBERY

It was a rainy morning in the late spring of 1885. Gray clouds hung low over the valley and shrouded the tops of the surrounding hills. An Overland stagecoach stood in front of the stage station in the gold mining town of Deadwood, deep in the heart of the Black Hills in the Dakota Territory. The six horses used to pull the heavy stagecoach seemed restless and anxious to get started on their long trek to the town of Spearfish.

Two men wearing slickers stepped out of the bank next to the stage station. They had hog-eared shotguns firmly gripped in their hands. They looked up and down the street before signaling to the bank teller that it was safe to come out.

Four more men came out of the bank. They were carrying a large wooden box with wide steel bands around it. On one side of the box was a heavy steel padlock. The four men loaded the box on the stagecoach while the two armed guards stood by.

Once the box was set in place on top of the stagecoach and secured with ropes, one of the guards climbed up onto the seat next to the driver. The other guard stood next to the coach and signaled for the ticket agent to let the passengers board.

There were three passengers on this gloomy morning, a woman and two men. The woman boarded the stage first with the aid of the guard. She wore a large brimmed hat with several long feathers flowing off the back, and a dress that fit her fine figure well. It was of a bright red material with a white lace collar. Her flared skirt covered several petticoats. She also carried a matching umbrella to keep the rain off.

The second passenger to board was a rather small man in a suit that had seen better days. The cuffs were worn and frayed. He wore an old Derby hat and spats that had been white at one time, but were stained from walking in the muddy streets. He carried a carpetbag and a small box that contained samples of his wares.

The third person to board was a hard looking man with a thick handlebar mustache and a long thin scar on his left cheek. His black hat was pulled down, and his dark eyes looked sinister under the brim. The collar of his slicker was turned up. Water dripped off his hat indicating that he had been standing out in the rain for some time. His boots were covered with mud. As he stepped up into the stagecoach, his slicker opened revealing the well-worn handle of his gun. He carried his gun low and tied down.

Once the three passengers were seated in the stagecoach, the second guard climbed inside. As soon as he was seated, he called up to the driver to move it out. The driver shouted at the horses and the heavy stagecoach lunged forward, rocking on its thick leather straps.

The sound of the horses' hooves as they splashed through the muddy streets filled the otherwise silent air. At the end of the street, the stagecoach turned and was soon on the Deadwood to Spearfish road.

As the stagecoach rocked and bounced along the road, no one inside said anything. The guard sat next to the woman. The man with the scar on his face sat next to the little man. It was the little man who first broke the silence.

"My name is Frederick Kerney," the little man said proudly as he tipped his hat and smiled at the woman.

She had not realized it, but she had been staring at the man with the scar on his face. The sudden sound of a voice startled her for a moment. She turned and looked at Mr. Kerney. She smiled politely, then nodded to acknowledge his introduction of himself, but did not say anything.

"I'm a traveling salesman," he continued when no one else offered to introduce themselves. "I sell barbed wire. The best barbed wire in the world."

"That's nice," the woman replied.

"May I ask what your name is, Miss?"

"Miss Jennifer Atwood," she answered without further comment.

She glanced back at the man with the scar in time to see him look away. She was sure that he had been watching her, but she had not caught him looking directly at her.

"What brings such a pretty lady as yourself to this part of the country?"

She looked back at Mr. Kerney and hesitated before she answered. "I'm going to Spearfish to teach at the new Black Hills College."

"A very honorable profession," he replied before turning to the man with the scar. "And what might your name be, sir?"

The man slowly turned his head and looked down at the little man. "My name might be Sam Talbot."

"The Sam Talbot? Marshall Sam Talbot?" Mr. Kerney asked with a note of excitement and surprise in his voice.

"I'm the only one I know of," Sam replied impatiently.

"Miss, we have the honor of being on the same stagecoach as the famous Marshall Sam Talbot. No one would dare rob this stagecoach, now. Why, he's gunned down..."

"Why don't you put a cork in it," Sam interrupted, his voice firm and harsh.

"Ah, yes sir," Mr. Kerney stuttered as he leaned back on the seat.

Miss Atwood looked from Talbot to Kerney, then back to Talbot. It was clear that Marshall Talbot's comment to Mr. Kerney had frightened the little man. She had heard stories about the Marshall, and how he had captured a gang of robbers. If she remembered correctly, he had been credited with killing all but two of the six robbers. All she could remember hearing about him was that he was a ruthless man who used his gun with great effectiveness.

The guard sitting across from Talbot looked at him. He had heard that there was going to be a marshal on the stagecoach soon, but he didn't know it was going to be on this trip, and that it was going to be Marshall Talbot.

The guard had heard about Marshall Talbot, but he had never met him. If this was Marshall Talbot, he was glad to have the extra gun should trouble occur. The stagecoach had been held up several times on this run in the past couple of months. Each time, the robbers got away with the strong box, and each time at least one guard had been killed.

"Excuse me, Marshall, but are you here to help us guard the strong box?"

Talbot looked up at the guard. He hesitated before answering with a quiet, but firm, "No."

"Then, why you are on this stagecoach?" the guard asked.

"That's really none of your business," he replied flatly.

The guard looked at Talbot for a second before turning toward the window. He drew back the curtain and looked outside.

It was still raining, although it was more of a mist than a rain. The low hanging clouds made for poor visibility as the stagecoach bounced along the rutted road.

The guard let the curtain drop back in place and sat back to relax. He glanced over at Marshall Talbot and wondered why he was on this stagecoach if it was not to help them protect the gold shipment.

It would be awhile before they would get to the narrowest part of the road, the part where the road ran along the bottom of Spearfish Canyon. In several places it was very narrow, while in others it ran through areas that were thick with trees and rocky outcroppings. The canyon was well suited for robbers to prey upon the lonely stagecoaches and other travelers that passed this way.

With Talbot's rebuke of the guard for asking too many questions still hanging in the air, the passengers took the hint and remained silent. No one had spoken for a long time. It was not out of respect that the passengers remained silent, but out of fear. Marshall Talbot's reputation as a man with a short temper, along with his reputation as a gunman, was enough to instill fear in the hearts and minds of almost anyone.

The passengers began to look at one another when they realized that the stagecoach was beginning to slow down. The stagecoach rocked to a stop. Everyone looked at Talbot as if they expected him to know why the stagecoach was stopping.

"This is where you wanted off, Marshall," the driver called down from his perch high on top of the stagecoach.

Talbot opened the door and stepped out of the stagecoach. Before he closed the door, he looked back at Miss Atwood for a moment. He reached up, lightly touched the brim of his hat and nodded slightly. He then closed the door.

"Get it out of here," Talbot called up to the driver.

The driver yelled at the horses and the stagecoach lunged forward. Talbot stood watching the stagecoach as it rolled on down the muddy road.

Jennifer had watched Marshall Talbot as he tipped the brim of his hat to her, then close the door. That simple sign of respect surprised her. She could not resist pushing back the curtain and looking out. She could see him standing alongside the road watching the stagecoach as it bounced along, leaving him behind.

She wondered why a man would get off a stagecoach out here in the middle of nowhere. It was then that her attention was drawn to movement in the trees just beyond Marshall Talbot. A lone rider came out of the trees leading a second horse that was saddled and ready to ride. She instantly wondered who the rider was, but lost sight of him before he reached Marshall Talbot.

As soon as she could no longer see him, she dropped the curtain and stared at the seat directly across from her where the Marshall had been sitting. She wondered where he might be going. It was clear that he had planned to meet someone out here, but why?

"Are you all right, Miss Atwood?"

She was startled by Mr. Kerney's question. The sound of his voice had interrupted her thoughts.

"Ah, Yes. Yes, I'm fine," she replied.

She glanced over at the guard only to discover that he was looking at her, too. Having them staring at her, made her feel rather uncomfortable.

"I'm fine, really," she said in the hope that they would quit looking at her and leave her to her thoughts.

For the next hour or so, the heavy Overland stagecoach rocked and bounced its way along the Deadwood to Spearfish road. It had stopped raining, but it remained overcast and misty. The only sounds that permeated the interior of the stagecoach were the sounds of the horses' hooves on the soft wet ground, and the splashing of the wheels through the mud puddles. There was also the occasional sound of the driver's voice as he encouraged his team on.

Suddenly, the sound of the driver's voice alerted everyone inside the stagecoach that something was wrong.

"Whoa. Whoa," the driver yelled as he pulled back on the reins of the horses and pushed hard on the brake arm with his foot. The rear wheels skidded in the slippery mud until the stagecoach came to a stop.

The guard suddenly sat up straight and looked at the other passengers. It was clear from the look on his face that this was not a normal stop.

He cautiously pushed the curtain to one side and peered out. He could not see anything. The stagecoach had come to a stop in one of the narrowest parts of the canyon. On one side was a cliff rising high above the stagecoach. On the other side was a rocky drop off of about ten feet to the creek below.

"What's goin' on? Why did we stop?" the guard called out.

"There's a tree across the road in front of us," the driver answered.

The guard on the top of the coach looked around, his eyes moving quickly from one spot to another. There was no doubt as to what was passing through his mind. The guard knew that this could very well be a trap. It was impossible for the stagecoach to get around the tree, and the trail was too narrow to turn the stagecoach around.

"We're going to have to move the tree," the guard up on top of the stagecoach called down to his partner.

The guard inside opened the door. As he started to get out, a shot rang out and he fell back into the stagecoach as his shotgun fell to the ground.

"Don't nobody move less'n you want to die," a voice from the trees called out.

The driver and the guard next to him looked around in an effort to see something, but the man was too well hidden among the rocks and trees.

"You, up on top, throw down the scattergun."

The guard did as he was told and dropped his shotgun. He knew that this was no time to put up a fight.

"Now, you and the driver climb down."

The driver wrapped the reins around the brake arm and climbed down along with the guard. They stood next to the stagecoach with their hands in the air.

Jennifer looked at the dead guard. She could not believe that this was happening. The poor man never had a chance.

"Everybody out. Now," the robber demanded.

Mr. Kerney did not wait to be told a second time. He had seen the guard shot to death without warning, and had no desire to end up just as dead. He got out of the stagecoach and put his hands up.

Jennifer did not move. The thought of having such ruthless men about without any protection filled her with fear, but she had little time to think about it. She reached down and took the guard's pistol. She slipped the gun in between the folds of her skirt and held it there as she climbed out of the stagecoach.

Once everyone was standing alongside the stagecoach, a man with a dark hat and black slicker came out from behind the trees. He was carrying a rifle. Within minutes, two others showed themselves. They were also carrying rifles and had handguns on their hips.

The driver recognized the robbers. The one in the dark hat and black slicker was Frank Parks. He was a ruthless man with a reputation for beating up anyone, man or woman, who stood in his way. He also had a reputation as a cold-blooded killer.

The skinny younger man was Slim Morris. How he got hooked up with a man like Parks was anybody's guess. He was known by many as a petty thief, but he had apparently graduated to robbing stagecoaches.

The third man was Billy Walker. He was not very bright and could be talked into almost anything. He never did anything without someone telling him what to do. Most of the time, he could be found cleaning up saloons in Spearfish or Sturgis.

"Well, what do we have here," Parks said with a grin as he approached Jennifer. "You're a pretty little thing."

"You leave her alone," the guard insisted.

Parks stopped, looked at Jennifer for a second or two, then with the swiftness of a rattlesnake he swung around and shot the guard in the stomach. The shock of seeing him shoot the guard so quickly startled Jennifer causing her to jump. She accidentally let go of the gun she had hidden in the folds of her skirt. It fell to the ground with a thud. Parks turned back to Jennifer when he heard the gun drop on the muddy ground.

"What did you plan to do with this, little lady," Parks said as he bent down and picked the gun up out of the mud.

"Come on, Frank. Let's just get the gold and get out of here," Slim said impatiently.

Parks just stood there looking Jennifer over. The way he looked at her, and the look on his face, made her very nervous and self-conscious. For the first time in her life, she felt really scared. Scared of what a man like him might do to her.

"What's your hurry, Slim?"

"There might be someone followin' 'um."

"There ain't nobody followin' 'um."

"That's what you think," Jennifer blurted out.

As soon as she said it, she wished that she had not. She really didn't know if Marshall Talbot and the other rider she had seen were following them. At this moment, she was secretly hoping that they were coming to their rescue.

"It seems the little lady thinks someone is comin' to save them. Now just who might that be, Missy?" Parks asked with a sinister grin.

"Marshall Talbot, that's who," she replied defiantly.

The smug look in Parks' face quickly disappeared. He stared into Jennifer's eyes in an effort to see if she was telling the truth or not. He had had a run-in with Marshall Talbot several years ago, and would not easily forget it.

"Get that strong box down," Parks ordered as he backed away from Jennifer so he could cover the rest of the passengers.

Slim leaned his rifle against the wheel of the stagecoach, then climbed up on top. He drew a knife from his belt and cut the ropes.

Parks was getting impatient. He kept looking from Jennifer to the top of the stagecoach. He still wasn't sure if she was telling the truth, but there was no sense wasting time that could prove valuable in getting away.

"Hurry it up," he demanded.

"Damn, Frank. This is heavy," Slim complained.

Parks looked over at Billy. He drew his pistol, then motioned to Billy.

"Get up there and help him."

Billy quickly leaned his rifle against a wheel and scampered up on top of the stagecoach. Between the two of them, they were able to push the strong box off the top of the stagecoach. It came crashing down onto the soft, wet ground with a thud.

As Slim and Billy quickly climbed down, Parks moved closer to the strong box. He waited until the two were down and had their guns on the passengers before he bent down and checked the padlock.

"Come on, Frank. Get it open," Slim demanded as his excitement to see what was in the box consumed him.

"Yeah, hurry up," Billy added excitedly.

"You shut up."

Parks took his gun and shot at the padlock. The first shot did not open the padlock, but the second shot broke it. He knelt down and opened the box.

"Why those...those..." Parks said as his mind slowly comprehended what he was seeing. He soon began to fill with rage.

Jennifer could see the surprised look on Parks' face as he stared into the strong box. She wondered what was wrong with him, and what he had seen in the strong box.

"What's wrong, Frank," Slim asked as he glanced toward Parks.

"There's nothin' in here but foul's gold," he screamed. "We've been set up, and Talbot's had a hand in it."

Suddenly a shot rang out and echoed down the canyon. Everybody froze. No one moved.

"Drop the gun, Parks. You're under arrest."

Parks looked around in an effort to see where Talbot was hiding. As his glance passed Jennifer, he realized that she had not been lying to him about Marshall Talbot coming to their rescue. It caused him to wonder about her. Was it possible that she had been in on this from the beginning?

"I said, drop the guns," Talbot demanded.

Suddenly, Slim lunged for his rifle, but a shot from behind some rocks quickly cut him down. Billy seemed to realize that the shot had not come from Marshall Talbot's position among the rocks.

"What do we do now," Billy asked as his excitement quickly turned to fear.

"Better do as he says, Billy. There's more than one of 'um," Parks whispered.

Without warning, Parks reached out and grabbed Jennifer by the arm. He jerked her in front of him and put his gun to her head. As he wrapped an arm around her narrow waist, he pulled her up against him.

"Talbot?"

"Yeah?"

"I'm not going to hang. You're going to let me go, or I'll kill the woman," Parks called out.

"You know I can't let you go."

"You don't have a choice. Are you ready to see this pretty little thing die?"

Talbot had Parks in the sights of his rifle, but quickly realized that there was too great a risk of hitting Miss Atwood if he tried to shoot Parks. He also knew that to simply wound Parks was not good enough. Parks was dangerous as long as he was alive.

"Hold your fire," Talbot called out reluctantly.

"Well, little lady, it looks like Marshall Talbot isn't as cold blooded as some give him credit. You stay as close to me as you are, or I'll kill you before he can get me. You understand?"

"Yes," she replied in a nervous whisper.

Parks began to slowly back up, pulling Jennifer along with him. He worked his way toward the back of the stagecoach, away from Marshall Talbot's line of fire.

Billy realized that Parks was going to leave him there. He did not want to be captured. He knew what the penalty for robbing a stagecoach and killing the guards would be. He did not want to face the gallows alone.

"You're not going to leave me here, are you?" Billy called desperately.

"You're on your own, kid," Parks said.

"I'm coming with you," Billy said and started to move toward Parks.

Suddenly, another shot rang out and a bullet ripped through Billy's leg. He fell to the ground in pain. The shot clearly disabled him. He was not going anywhere now.

"Damn, they shot me," Billy cried.

"Parks, you're making this tough on yourself," Marshall Talbot called out.

"Hell, they can only hang me once. What have I got to lose?"

"Let her go," Talbot demanded.

"Not on your life."

As Parks backed away from the stagecoach, he dragged Jennifer in front of him. Talbot was trying to decide what he should do. In the past, he had always simply shot the criminal. On two occasions, however, that had proven not to be the best choice. Once he hit the victim by accident, killing him. The other time, he caused permanent injury to the victim. He did not want that to happen to Miss Atwood.

Talbot slowly moved out from behind the cover of the trees toward the stagecoach as Parks moved away from it. Talbot could see the fear in Jennifer's eyes as Parks continued to drag her toward the brush where they had hidden their horses.

"I can't let you go, Parks," Talbot said as he took aim at Parks.

"You pull that trigger and this here pretty little lady is goin' to die," Parks warned him.

Talbot hesitated. The look on Miss Atwood's face was that of sheer terror. He wanted to help her, but how could he as long as Parks was using her as a shield. He would never forgive himself if he accidentally shot her.

Jennifer was afraid that Talbot was going to shoot, but was also afraid that he wouldn't. She would have to hold very still if Talbot was to get a good shot at Parks. When she saw Talbot slowly lower his rifle, she was both relieved and disappointed.

As Parks started to drag Jennifer backward up a rocky slope, she stumbled on the rocks causing them to fall to the ground. Parks held onto her. She saw Talbot quickly raise his rifle to his shoulder, but slowly lowered it again as she felt the barrel of Parks' gun press against the side of her head.

"I wouldn't stumble again if I was you, little lady. The next time might be fatal."

Talbot kept his rifle pointed at Parks, just in case he made a mistake and let up for one second. All he needed was one clear shot at him.

Talbot continued to follow Parks, forcing him to keep Miss Atwood in front of him. He tried to keep the pressure on Parks in the hope that he would make a mistake, and he could take him.

"You better back off, Talbot, or I'll kill her," Parks yelled.

"You hurt her and I'll cut you down before you know what happened," Talbot countered angrily.

Parks dragged Jennifer to the edge of the rocks. He held her in front of him as he took several quick glances to the sides and behind him. He then looked at Talbot for a moment.

Talbot was wondering what was going on in Parks' mind. He had stayed as close to Parks as he could in order to get a good shot at him if he so much as slipped again. He was a good fifteen feet away from Parks when he noticed that Parks had stopped backing up.

Parks was still looking at Talbot when he suddenly pushed Jennifer toward him. As Jennifer fell forward, Parks jumped down behind the rocks.

Talbot was surprised by Parks' sudden move. He lunged forward to catch Miss Atwood. As she stumbled down the slope, she began to lose her balance. Just as she was about to fall, Talbot dropped his rifle and caught her. Together they fell to the ground. Miss Atwood landing on top of Talbot. He quickly rolled over on her to protect her from Parks.

Talbot quickly drew his gun and looked back up the slope. He was ready to shoot, but there was no one there. He looked back at Miss Atwood.

"Are you all right, Ma'am?" he asked.

"I will be when you get off me," she replied.

Talbot sat up. He was embarrassed that he had not been gentler with her.

"I'm sorry, Miss. I was only trying to protect you."

"Yes, I know. Thank you, but don't you think you should go after him?"

"Yes, of course," he said sheepishly.

Talbot got up and ran back toward the stagecoach. At first, Jennifer wondered where he was going, because Parks had gone the other way. She quickly realized that he was going after a horse.

Talbot grabbed the reins of his horse and swung up into the saddle. He kicked the horse in the ribs and it jumped forward. His horse jumped over the tree that had stopped the stagecoach and raced on down the road.

Jennifer watched him as he disappeared down the road. She had no idea where he was going. She looked toward the stagecoach and saw the man Talbot had met back on the trail. He was standing guard over Billy.

"Aren't you going to help the Marshall?" she asked as she came around from the back of the stagecoach.

"No," Jesse replied calmly.

"But he may need your help."

"Not this time. This is his fight."

Jennifer turned and looked down the trail in the direction that Talbot had gone. She wasn't sure how she felt, but she knew that she was worried about him.

Talbot had a pretty good idea where Parks was headed. The trail that ran behind the rocks was an old logging road that had not been used for several years. It came out just a short way down the road. Talbot pushed his horse hard in an effort to beat Parks to the junction.

Talbot raced down the road, ducking branches and splashing through the creek as the road wondered through the canyon. As he came around a corner, he saw Parks come out of the trees and head down the road. The chase was on.

Parks caught a glimpse of Talbot and whipped his horse on. He drew his gun and tried to at least slow Talbot down by shooting back over his shoulder at him.

Talbot rode low on his horse and pressed his pursuit of Parks. He was slowly gaining on him.

As Parks' horse splashed into the creek, it stumbled and fell dumping Parks in the cold water. Just as he was getting up, he saw Talbot's horse rushing toward him. He reached for his gun, but it was gone.

Talbot rode his horse into the creek. As the horse ran past Parks, Talbot jumped off and tackled Parks. Both of them went tumbling into the water. Talbot was on his feet first. As Parks came up, Talbot met him with a hard right hook to the jaw. Parks' head twisted to the side as he fell backwards.

Parks staggered to get up, but Talbot hit him again smashing his nose flat against his face. Parks again fell backwards into the creek.

When Parks did not get up, Talbot waded up to him. As he reached down to pull Parks to his feet, Parks grabbed a rock from the creek bottom and swung it at Talbot's head. Talbot saw it just in time to duck the full force of the blow, but was struck with a glancing blow to the cheek. The blow dazed Talbot for a second causing him to fall to his hands and knees in the creek.

Parks was able to get to his feet first and began kicking Talbot in the ribs. Each kick sent a rush of pain through Talbot's side. On the third kick, Talbot was able to grab Parks by the leg and knock him off balance.

Talbot rolled over on top of Parks and began hitting him in the face and alongside the head. When Parks was no longer able to fight back, Talbot stopped hitting him.

Slowly, Talbot stood up and looked down at Parks. He was breathing hard, and his ribs hurt with each breath he took. He reached down and grabbed Parks by the collar and dragged him out of the creek. After retrieving his gun, Talbot sat down on a rock to catch his breath. Parks lay on the ground near the rock. He was out cold.

Talbot's thoughts were interrupted by the sound of the stagecoach coming down the road. He watched it as the driver stopped the stagecoach, but didn't get up. He was too winded and his ribs were hurting from the kicking he had received from Parks.

Jennifer was the first one to get out of the stagecoach. She hurried to Talbot and saw the cuts on his face.

"You're hurt," she said as she took her lacy handkerchief from her pocket.

"I'll be fine, Miss Atwood," he said.

She dipped her handkerchief in the cool clear water of the creek, then knelt down in front of Marshall Talbot. She gently dabbed the blood from the wound on his cheek.

"Thank you, Miss, but that's not necessary," Talbot said as he looked into her eyes.

"It's the least I can do for the man who saved my life," she replied softly.

Talbot did not know what to say. He found her very attractive and wondered what she saw in him.

"Let me help you to the stagecoach," she said.

"I can make it, Miss Atwood."

"Call me Jennifer, please," she said with a smile.

"Thank you, Jennifer," he said as he let her put her arm around him.

Talbot did not need any help, but he didn't mind having her arm around him. He put his arm around her shoulder and let her lead him to the stagecoach.

Once inside the stagecoach, Jennifer sat beside him. She held his hand.

Talbot glanced out the window. Jesse was tying Parks over the saddle of his horse. Knowing that Parks was captured gave Talbot a sense of relief, and allowed him to relax a little.

He turned back and looked at Jennifer. She smiled softly at him. Talbot glanced down and looked at her small delicate hand holding his rough callused hand. He did not know why she was still holding his hand, but he didn't mind.

"Would you consider me too forward if I asked if I could call on you when you get settled in Spearfish?" he asked as he looked at her.

"Not at all. I would be delighted to have you call on me."

They sat quietly, only occasionally speaking softly to each other as they continued their journey to Spearfish.

TO DIE TOO YOUNG

It was shortly after noon when I arrived in the dusty little town of Two Buttes in the southeastern corner of the Colorado Territory. It was a hell of a hot day with the sun beating down on the hard dry ground. I tied my horse in the shade of an old cottonwood tree next to a water trough, took off the saddle, then went into the Red Horse Saloon for a beer.

I would have preferred a nice quiet place to sleep, but it was just too hot to sleep. Instead, I looked for a quiet table in the back of the saloon where I could lean back and relax. After dark I could move on west in the cool of the night. There would be a full moon tonight, making it easy to travel.

I stopped at the bar for a beer, then took it to a table and sat down. I was minding my own business, drinking the lukewarm beer, when a young wrangler came busting in the front door like he owned the place. I casually looked up from my glass.

He was a tall, skinny kid with blond hair that flowed out from under his wide brimmed, flattop hat with its silver hatband. His clothes were dusty as if he had ridden a long way. He didn't look like he was hardly old enough to shave, not much older than, maybe sixteen or seventeen.

He stood in the door as he looked around the saloon. When he saw me, he hesitated a second before stepping up to the bar.

"Give me a beer," he demanded loudly as he slammed his fist down on the bar.

I wasn't sure just what this kid's problem was, but he was making it a point of letting the whole world know that he was here. I got the impression he thought he was the top dog in town and everyone should stay out of his way.

I watched as the barkeep poured a beer and set it down on the bar in front of him, then backed away. I noticed that the barkeep didn't take his eyes off him. From the look on the barkeep's face, I got the feeling he was afraid of this kid. Something told me that this was not the first time this young wrangler had been in here. That thought caused me to look him over a little more carefully.

The kid looked no different than any other young wrangler right off the range, except for two things. The first was how he wore his gun. He wore it low on his hip, almost on his leg, and he had it tied down.

The second was his gun. It was one of those fancy silver-plated Colt .45 Peacemakers, a fairly new gun to these parts. I'd seen only one like it before in Kansas City. It was an expensive gun. Not many young wranglers could afford one. I wondered where a kid like him got it. I also wondered if he knew how to use it, or if it was just a bit of flash he carried to make people think he was some sort of big shot.

I watched the young man take a sip of the beer. Almost instantly, he spit it out and slammed the glass down on the bar.

"I wanted a cold beer, not this warmed over horse piss. Get me a cold one."

"I can't," the barkeep said, hoping not to upset the kid.

"Then you get me something else that's cold or you'll wish you had," the kid said in a threatening tone.

"I ain't got no ice to keep things cold," the barkeep explained nervously.

I had heard about people being unreasonable, but this kid was downright nasty. Any fool would know there was no way anyone was going to get a cold beer out here in the middle of nowhere this time of year.

I've never been one to stick my nose into other people's business, but this young wrangler was getting on my nerves. I was hot and tired. I wasn't asking for much, just a little peace and quiet before I started out on the trail again. I didn't need to listen to this damn fool kid throw his weight around and belly ache about warm beer.

"Kid?"

I watched him turn around and look toward me. I could see he was sizin' me up.

"You talking to me, mister?"

"Do you see any other kid in this place?"

I could see that calling him a kid didn't set too well with him, but I didn't care. He was acting like a kid, so to my way of thinking he must be a kid.

"I ain't no kid, mister."

"Then quit actin' like one."

"I ain't actin' like one," he countered angrily.

"Listen, boy. I ain't goin' to sit here and argue with you. If you can't sit down and shut up, then at least shut up."

It was clear it angered him that I had the nerve to tell him what to do, but I was too hot and sweaty to care what he thought. I watched him step away from the bar, plant his feet firmly apart and shrug his shoulder as he readied himself to draw that fancy Colt. I watched his eyes. I could see his hand slowly move closer to his gun.

"You ain't tellin' me what to do, Mister."

This kid was brave enough, but stupid. He didn't know me, and I didn't know him, but I'd been around long enough to know his type. I'd seen kids like him die too young because they picked a fight with the wrong man, and wouldn't back off when they found themselves in over their heads.

"Kid, if you want to live to see the sun rise tomorrow mornin', you best rethink what's goin' on in your head."

His hand stopped moving as he looked at me. I could see he was mulling over what I had said in that thick skull of his. The fact that I didn't seem to be afraid of him must have given him cause to stop and think. Something he had failed to do up to now.

This kid was not smart enough to realize I had only one hand on top of the table that stood between us. My other hand was under the table. It was easy for anyone with half a brain to see that if he didn't change his ways, he might very well die right here, right now. The last thing I wanted to do was to kill this kid, but if he continued he was going to push me to the point where he would give me no choice.

"Listen kid, there's a .44 under this table pointed right at your belly. I suggest you turn around, stand up to the bar and quietly drink your beer. When you're finished with it, leave. I don't want to hear another sound come out of your mouth."

Before I finished telling him what to do, he was looking down at the table. He began to realize there was a good possibility that I had the drop on him. The look on his face suddenly changed from one of complete confidence in himself to fear.

I watched his face turn pale. I'm sure he was convinced that he was only seconds from being dead if he didn't do as he was told. I could see the sweat break out on his forehead as he slowly raised his empty hands and began to back up to the bar.

He slowly turned around, picked up his beer and drank it down without stopping. When he was done, he set the glass back down on the bar and slowly turned to look at me again. I still had one hand under the table. His eyes drifted up from the table. He was still not sure if I had the drop on him, but he wasn't going to take the chance. He turned toward the door and began walking toward it. Just before he stepped outside, he glanced back toward me one more time. I got the feeling that this was not going to be the end of this.

When he was out the door, I leaned back and let out a sigh of relief. I moved my hand out from under the table just as the barkeep came over with another beer. He noticed my hand was empty.

"You was takin' a hell of a chance pullin' a bluff like that on him," the barkeep said. "He ain't one to be forgettin' you put him down."

"You know the kid?"

"Yeah. His old man's a big shot up around Cheyenne Wells. Owns a lot of land and cattle up that way."

"What's the kid doin' way down here?" I asked.

"He comes down this way a couple times a year. I think he goes down to Texas to buy cattle, then moves the herds up to their place usin' an old trail some miles east of here."

"Well, he may be angry now, but at least he's alive," I reminded the barkeep.

"When you leave here, you be sure to take care. I wouldn't trust him. It'd be just like him to be waitin' for you down the road."

"Thanks for the advice. And thanks for the beer."

The barkeep nodded, then went back behind the bar. I sat and thought about what the barkeep had said. I wondered if the kid would try to bushwhack me. Even though we were going in different directions, it wouldn't hurt to keep my eyes open. There was no telling what he might try next.

I relaxed as best I could during the heat of the afternoon. I sipped on lukewarm beer as the time slowly passed. Over the next few hours I went out and checked on my horse a couple of times. I fed him and made sure that he had plenty of water.

While I waited for night to come, I noticed that only a couple of people came into the saloon for a drink. None of them stayed very long.

I watched the sun set from my chair in the saloon. As the barkeep walked around the saloon lighting a few of the lamps, I noticed a slight breeze creep in through the open door. It felt fresh and smelled clean. It was getting on toward time to leave.

I pushed back my chair and stood up. The barkeep looked over at me as I stretched.

"You goin'?" he asked.

"Yeah. I think I'll get on down the trail. Thanks for the company, and the beers."

"You're welcome, and come back again. Remember what I told you, you be careful out there."

"Sure will," I replied and walked out of the saloon.

I went across the street to the big cottonwood and saddled my horse. As soon as I was ready, I swung up into the saddle and looked around. The town was quiet, but I was sure that it was like this most of the time.

I nudged my horse in the ribs and he started down the road. He seemed to be glad that we had waited until it cooled some before starting out again. I know I was. I made it a point to keep my eyes and ears open. I took to heart the warning from the barkeep.

Once out of town, I glanced up at the stars. The tiny specks of light seemed to fill the sky. I noticed back to the east the moon was just starting to come up over the horizon. This was open country out here, broken up only by a few gullies and ravines that cut across the otherwise flat land. What few hills there were rolled gently over the land.

As I came to one of those gullies, my horse felt his way down the steep side to the bottom. He then started up the other side. It was a rather steep embankment, but a fairly short one. I nudged him on up the slope with a gentle kick in the ribs.

Just as we reached the top, a shot rang out and I felt a sudden pain in my side. I fell backwards off my horse and hit the ground with a bone-jarring thud, which almost knocked the wind out of me.

It took a second or two for it to register in my mind what had happened, but the burning pain in my left side made it all too clear very quickly. I had been shot, and I had no idea how badly I was hurt. I could not see anything in the dark. The shot must have spooked my horse, as he was nowhere in sight.

I found myself in the dark shadows of the gully. Even though I could not see how bad my wound was, at least the bushwhacker could not see me.

I drew my gun from my holster with my right hand, then passed it to my left. I reached across my body and lightly touched my left side in an effort to find out how badly I was hurt. Touching my wound sent a sharp pain through me. I could feel the moist blood on my shirt, and quickly realized that I needed to do something to stop the bleeding.

I lay quietly and listened to see if the coward that had ambushed me was still around. When I heard nothing, I laid my gun on the ground at my side and took my bandanna from around my neck. I gently stuffed it under my shirt over the wound in the hope of stopping the bleeding.

After picking up my gun, I laid back and took a deep breath. I waited and listened. I had no idea if my attacker was still around just waiting for me to let him know that I was alive, or if he had run off thinking that he had done his deed.

I decided it was best if I laid low and stayed quiet for awhile. If he had decided that I might not be dead, he might show himself in an effort to find out. It was clear to me that I was in no condition to go after him.

Time passed slowly. I could hear nothing moving. There was a gentle breeze, but not enough to ruffle the short grass along the edge of the gully. I waited.

Suddenly, I heard a strange sound. It sounded like a horse munching on grass. I looked along the edge of the gully, but saw nothing. I tried to prepare myself for whatever might be out there.

My horse suddenly appeared in the moonlight on the top of the gully. He was slowly moving along the edge, eating the tender grass. I thought about calling to him in the hope of getting him to come back down into the gully, but that would let my enemy know I was still alive. I wasn't sure if I could crawl up the side of the gully and get to him, so I decided to lie quietly for awhile longer.

As I watched my horse only a few yards away, I wondered who had shot me. Of course, my thoughts quickly turned to the young hot head I had words with in the Red Horse Saloon earlier in the day. I remembered what the barkeep had said about him. I couldn't think of anyone else who would want me dead.

I glanced up at my horse as he stood above the gully. His head came up abruptly, and his ears pointed down along the gully. He had heard something I had not. I checked my gun to make sure it was ready, then readied myself. I listened in an effort to hear what my horse had heard, but heard nothing at first. I watched my horse as he started to move away from the gully.

Then I heard something. It sounded like stones and dirt rolling down the side of the gully. I quickly realized that something, or someone, had slid down the embankment into the gully to my right. I shifted around until I was in a better position to see someone coming toward me from that direction. It was not easy to move with the pain in my side.

I carefully listened as I cocked the hammer back on my old Remington Army .44 caliber. As the hammer set, it gave out a clicking noise that could be heard for several yards in the stillness of the night air. I laid still and listened, but heard nothing. If my enemy had heard me cock my gun, he would know I was alive and he would be wary.

"Well, well. You're still alive. I was beginning to think I killed you with one shot. That would've disappointed me. I want you to know who shot you before you die."

I immediately recognized the voice as that of the kid in the Red Horse Saloon. The tone of his voice indicated that he knew he had the upper hand at the moment. The arrogance in his voice angered me. I wanted to yell at him that I was a long way from being dead, but I kept silent.

"I know you're hurt bad. How's it feel to be slowly bleeding to death out here in the middle of nowhere?"

Even though he kept talking in an effort to get me to say something, I was not about to give away my position. I had seen young gunslingers like him before. They are consumed with their own importance. They always grow impatient and can't wait to see what they've done. I would bide my time and wait, besides I was in no condition to escape. My best, and probably only hope of surviving this, was to lie still until he decided to move in closer to find out if I was finally dead.

"You're not going to make this easy for me, are you?"

I wanted to tell him that I planned to make it as hard on him as I could. I also wanted to tell him what a coward I thought he was, but to talk could be the end for me. He was young, healthy and pretty good with a gun. I was older, more experienced, but wounded. The only thing I had going for me was patience.

I didn't move. I kept my eyes moving in the hope of seeing him before he saw me. A shadow, the sound of his boot in the loose dirt, any little thing that would warn me that he was getting closer.

Suddenly, I heard something move. I raised my gun and pointed it in the direction of the noise. Holding it as steady as I could, I sighted down the barrel.

I got a glimpse of something shiny, like the moonlight was reflecting off something. I aimed just to one side and below the reflection, then slowly pulled the trigger. My gun gave out a loud bang as it jumped in my hand. The muzzle flash briefly lit up an area close to the embankment. Almost instantly, there was another flash of light and the sound of another shot. A bullet slammed into the embankment above my head, raining dirt down on me.

At the same time, I heard the soft muffled sound of someone in pain. I instantly knew I had hit the kid, but I couldn't tell how seriously he was wounded. I could have injured him just enough to make him mad, or I could have almost killed him. There was no way for me to know in the dark. I waited and listened.

"I'll be damned. You got me," I heard him say almost as if he had not been shot at all.

There was a tone of surprise in his voice. By the way he said it, and the sound of his voice, I knew he had come here to simply kill me for running him out of the saloon. I don't think he thought for a second that things might not work out the way he thought they should.

"You asked for it, kid. How's it feel to be slowly bleeding to death out here in the middle of nowhere?" I said, reminding him that he had asked me that very same question just a few minutes ago.

I continued to listen for some movement, but heard nothing for a long while. I began to wonder what was going on in his mind.

"You weren't supposed to shoot me. It wasn't supposed to work out this way," the kid said.

"Sorry, kid, but what the hell was I supposed to do, let you kill me without a fight?"

"It burns like hell."

"Sure does. Never been shot before?"

There was a long silence before he answered.

"No."

"You hurt bad, kid?"

"Don't know."

"Why'd you pick on me?"

"I ain't never been run out of a saloon like that before."

Although he answered me, I could hear the pain in his voice.

"Well, you was askin' for it."

There was another long period of silence before he said anything more.

"There's somethin' I gotta know. Was you holdin' a gun under that table?"

I hesitated to answer him, but decided he had a right to know. After all, what difference did it make now?

"No."

"You bluffed me," he said with surprise. "I could've killed yah right there."

"Maybe, maybe not," I replied.

We didn't say anything for quite a spell. I just laid there and listened. I heard him cough a little. It sounded like he was trying to cover it up, but I could still hear him. It would be a shame for a young man to die so young out here, especially for no reason.

"You doin' okay, kid?" I asked.

"You know, there's a hell... of a lot of stars... up there."

I looked up at the sky, but I couldn't help but think about this young kid. He had dealt out the cards, and from the sound of his voice, he didn't get too good a hand. My bullet must have done some serious damage. I noticed the difficulty he seemed to be having in completing a sentence without taking a break to breathe.

"That moon looks pretty big tonight, too."

I didn't know what else to say. I thought about crawling toward him to check and see if I could help him. But if he was playing games with me that might be just what he wanted me to do.

"Hey, kid. What's your name?"

"Jesse. What's yours?"

"Sam. Where you from?"

"Cheyenne Wells. You?"

"Around."

I didn't know what else to do but exchange a bit of small talk. If it made him feel better, that was good. Besides, as long as he was talking, I knew he wasn't sneaking up on me.

"You got family up that way?"

"Yeah, but what...do you care?"

"Just wonderin'. I guess when you get right down to it, I really don't care, kid."

The pain in my side was turning into a dull ache making it uncomfortable for me to remain like I was. I decided that I needed to move in order to make myself more comfortable. As I moved, I shook loose some dirt that slid down the slope of the gully.

"What you doin'?" the kid asked.

He sounded suddenly frightened, as if he thought I was coming after him.

"Nothing. I'm just trying to get more comfortable."

"Oh."

"How you feelin', kid?"

"I'm getting a little cold," he said softly. "Must be the night air."

The night air was warm and dry. This was one of those nights when you could sleep on top of your bedroll and not get cold.

"Say kid, you still hurtin'?"

"Not so much... any more. I got just a dull...ache, sort of."

I heard him cough a couple of times. I was sure he was in pretty bad shape by now. I leaned back and looked up at the sky again. In my mind, I knew this kid was on his way out.

"Mister?"

"Yeah?"

"Do you suppose we could...call this off?" he asked.

The sound of his voice seemed to be getting weaker. In my heart, I was sure he didn't have much time left.

"That would suit me just fine."

"Good. I'm gettin' really tired."

"Me, too."

I let out a sigh, then listened to see if he was moving. I didn't hear anything. I tried to relax and make myself as comfortable as possible. I kept my gun in my hand, just in case.

Time passed slowly. I watched the moon slowly move up in the sky. My horse had returned to the edge of the gully. I spent a few minutes watching him eat the grass. He seemed undisturbed by what was going on in the gully below him. Then it hit me. My horse had wondered off when he heard something in the gully. Now that it was silent, he was back.

"Hey, kid?" I said, but there was no answer.

I called to him again, but still no answer. Something deep inside me told me that he was dead. I closed my eyes and let sleep rest my body.

When the sun came up, I woke to find my horse still standing above the gully. I looked to my right. Not more than a few yards away laid the young wrangler. The front of his shirt, just above his belt buckle, was covered with a large dark spot. It was clear that he was dead. His fancy gun was lying beside him.

I crawled out of the gully and pulled myself up onto the back of my horse, but not without some difficulty and a lot of discomfort. I looked back down into the gully at the kid, then turned my horse back toward Two Buttes.

When I got back to town, I told the barkeep at the Red Horse Saloon what had happened while he dressed my wound. He did not seem surprised.

After he finished taking care of my wound, he helped me to his back room so I could rest.

"What about the kid? Shouldn't someone go get him?"

"I'll take care of that," the barkeep said. "You rest."

I watched the barkeep leave the room. My thoughts turned to the kid. He was dead. He died too young, and for no reason.

REVENGE

It was the summer of 1867 in the Dakota Territory. The morning was unusually cold and overcast as Jacob Henry left his sod house and walked toward the barn. It was a day that was much like the feelings that churned inside him, dark and gloomy.

Once inside the barn, Jacob led his horse out of the stall and put a bridle on it. He threw his saddle up on the back of the horse and pulled the cinch tight around the horse's belly. After putting his saddlebags on and sliding his rifle into the scabbard, he led the horse out of the barn. Putting his foot in the stirrup, he swung his leg over the saddle and sat down.

He sat looking over the small ranch he was about to leave behind and might never see again. He looked at the sod house he had built for his wife and son. Like many others, they had come out west after the Civil War in the hope of starting a new life.

Slowly, his eyes moved toward the two new graves under an old cottonwood tree. No tears came to his eyes as he thought about his wife and son whom he had buried there only yesterday. His only feeling was to get revenge against those who had killed them.

There had been no preacher to say soft, kind words over their graves. There were no neighbors to come and console him in his time of sorrow. He had done his crying alone in the quiet of the night. Now it was time for him to find their killers, and to see that they paid for what they had done.

Out on the prairie there were few laws and fewer lawmen to enforce what laws did exist. Just staying alive from day to day was hard enough for most men. When justice was needed, it was up to the individual to dispense justice as best he could. But Jacob was not interested in justice. He wanted revenge.

When Jacob had returned from the trading post at Fort Pierre, he found his wife and son dead. He also found the tracks of three horses and the footprints of three men in front of his house. He could not wait any longer. If he was to catch the men, he would have to leave now. Jacob Henry pulled on the reins of his horse, turned away from the house and road away.

For the next several days, he followed the tracks of the three men across the wide-open prairie. Stopping to take a rest and to check for tracks, he stepped out of the saddle and knelt down. On the ground were three sets of hoof prints in the soft earth. The marks in the dirt left by one of the horse's shoes quickly reassured him that he was still on the right trail. The left front horseshoe of one of the horses had a V-shaped notch in it. He also noticed that one of the horses had developed a slight limp.

The three sets of hoof prints told him that the three men he had been following had not split up. They were still riding together and still headed east. From the looks of the trail they left behind, they seemed to have a destination in mind, but Jacob had no idea where they might be going.

Jacob stood up and stretched as he looked out across the vast emptiness of the prairie. For the first time, he began to feel that he was getting closer. It would not be long before he would have to face them, but he was ready.

He mounted up and continued on across the prairie. The thought that he might be getting closer gave him new energy. He had no idea where they were going, but it didn't matter. He would follow them, no matter where they went.

If his memory served him right, there was a small town just a few miles up ahead. As he followed the trail, he was sure he would pass within a stone's throw of it. Maybe someone there would be able to help him find the men he was looking for.

The trail of the three men led into the small dreary town of Faulkton on the south fork of Snake Creek. It was not much of a town. There was a small whitewashed church, a saloon, a general store, a livery stable and a boardinghouse.

Jacob rode across the creek and down the dirt street of the town. As he rode, he kept looking around. He wasn't sure who he was looking for, but he was sure he would know them when he saw them.

It was a quiet little town. There were only two horses tied in front of the general store. He looked them over carefully as he rode toward the livery stable. The local blacksmith greeted him as he dismounted.

"Howdy."

"Howdy. You got room for my horse?"

"Sure do. Got one stall left. Looks like you come a ways, Mister?"

"I have. Have you seen three riders pass this way in, say, the last day or so?"

"Yeah, sure did. They friends?"

"No. Do you know which way they went?"

"They're still here in town. I have their horses. One of them's lame, but should be better in a day or two."

That bit of information caused Jacob's heart to jump and his chest to tighten. He was unable to describe his feelings at that moment, but he knew that the time was at hand when he would confront them. They were here, and here was where he would get his revenge.

"You all right?" the Blacksmith asked as he noticed the strange look on Jacob's face.

"Yeah. Is there someplace I can get a good meal?"

"Over at the boardinghouse or at the saloon. The saloon puts up a mighty fine meal."

"Thanks," Jacob said as he slid his rifle out of the scabbard.

Tucking his rifle in the crook of his arm, he walked across the street to the saloon. As he entered the saloon, he noticed a man standing at the bar. He was not a farmer. From the buckskins the man wore, he looked like he might be a trapper, or buffalo hunter.

Jacob walked across the room to a table in the corner and sat down with his back to the wall. He looked around the saloon, but saw no one else except the barkeep.

Jacob studied the man in the buckskins for several minutes. The man wore high top moccasins and carried his gun low on his hip, along with a big knife. Jacob also noticed a small piece of ribbon tied to the handle of his knife. It was the same color, and the same kind of ribbon his wife had used in her hair. Jacob was convinced that this man was one of the men he was hunting, but he had to be sure.

Jacob laid his rifle on the table with the barrel pointing toward the man at the bar. He then put both hands on the table where they could be seen. He took a deep breath, he was ready. He called out to the man.

"You. You in the buckskins."

The man at the bar slowly turned and looked at Jacob. He was obviously sizing up Jacob. He saw the rifle on the table, but Jacob's hands were not on it.

"You talking to me, Mister?" the man asked as his eyes narrowed.

"Yeah. I'm Jacob Henry. Does that name mean anything to you?"

"No. Can't say that it does. Should it?" the man asked sharply.

Jacob knew he was pressing this man. It was important to Jacob that he make the first move.

"I would think you would find out the names of the people you kill, especially when they are a defenseless woman and a small child."

The man looked at Jacob for a second. He could see Jacob's muscles tense. Suddenly, his eyes grew big and his jaw dropped. Jacob watched the man as he straightened up and firmly set his feet. It was only a matter of seconds before the man would draw his gun.

"Barkeep, this is a man who kills women and children. I suggest you step aside," Jacob warned.

Suddenly, the man dropped his shoulder as he reached for his gun. Jacob reached over and dropped his hand over his rifle. His finger swiftly gripped the trigger and pulled. The man's gun barely cleared his holster, when the deafening sound of Jacob's rifle going off filled the room along with the smell of gunpowder.

The slug from Jacob's rifle caught the man square in the chest and slammed him back against the bar. His eyes filled with a look of surprise and terror. He looked at Jacob for a second or two, then looked down at the front of his shirt. The dark colored spot on his shirt grew larger with each passing second.

The man looked up at Jacob again as his gun slipped from his fingers and fell to the floor. As his eyes closed, the man's knees buckled and he fell to the floor, dead.

Jacob stood up and looked down at the dead man. He was not sorry that he had killed him. Deep down in the recesses of his mind, Jacob knew this was just the beginning. He had killed one, but there were still two others.

Jacob heard the sound of someone running along the boardwalk in front of the saloon. He turned and looked toward the door just as a man came charging into the saloon.

Jacob swung his rifle around, but he was too late. The man had a gun in his hand and fired a wild shot at him. The bullet grazed Jacob's left arm, causing him to drop his rifle. Jacob was about to draw his gun from his holster when he heard someone else running toward the saloon.

The first man through the door had scrambled for cover behind a table. Jacob quickly realized he was in no position to fight both of them. His only chance for surviving was to get away. He turned and dove through a window.

Jacob scrambled to his feet, then ran along the side of the saloon and turned down the alley. Just as he turned the corner, he heard a gunshot and a bullet slammed into the corner of the general store, splintering the wood and sending pieces of it into the air.

Jacob ran down the alley toward the creek. When he got to the creek, he dropped down behind a big cottonwood tree and hid in the tall grass at the base of the tree. He checked to see if anyone was following him as he tried to catch his breath. No one was coming, at least not at the moment. He knew it wouldn't be long before they would come for him.

The pain in his arm reminded him that he had been shot. He had to do something to stop the bleeding. Using his teeth and one hand, he was able to tie his neckerchief tightly over the wound in his arm. Once it was secure, he laid down at the base of the tree to wait, and to watch.

It wasn't long before he saw two men coming down the alley. They were moving cautiously, being careful to look around corners, behind barrels and in doorways.

While watching them slowly move toward him, Jacob took careful aim at the bigger of the two men. He held the man in the sights of his pistol, but did not pull the trigger. He knew he would have just one shot at him. Patiently, he waited and watched as they moved closer and closer.

Slowly, Jacob pulled back the hammer on his gun. He could feel the burning sensation in his arm and the sweat roll down his face. He blinked as he slowly squeezed the trigger.

Just as the big man saw Jacob, the gun jumped in his hand and the deafening sound of his gun going off echoed off the walls of the buildings. As the smoke and the noise settled down, Jacob could see the big man doubled over. He was holding his stomach as he staggered backward then fell to the ground.

Jacob found it difficult to keep his eyes off the man as he fell, but the sudden sound of gunfire, and the sound of a bullet ripping through a tree branch near his head, caused him to duck down behind the tree. Then, it was quiet.

Jacob listened and waited, but he heard nothing. Slowly, he rose up and looked out from behind the cottonwood tree. All he could see was the big man lying in the dirt, curled up on his side clutching his stomach.

He had gut shot the big man. If the man was not already dead, he would most likely be dead by nightfall. Jacob slowly stood up next to the tree. He looked around for the last of the three, but when he didn't see him, he walked toward the big man lying on the ground. Kneeling down beside him, he looked at the man. It was easy to see the fear of death in the man's eyes. He knew that he was going to die.

"Where's your friend?" Jacob asked sharply.

"I....don't...know," his voice filled with pain.

"You killed my wife and son."

"Please...Mister. Don't...let...me...die... like...this."

"Where did he go," Jacob insisted.

"I.... don't...know," the big man insisted.

Jacob looked up. He saw several of the town folks walking toward him. They seemed to be cautious, afraid that the shooting might not be over. They looked at Jacob as if he were a ruthless gunman who killed for pleasure, but Jacob did not care what they thought. They did not know what these men had done to his family. These people had no way of understanding what was happening here, and they were not in a position to judge him.

He heard the sound of a horse running down the street in front of the buildings. Jacob turned in time to catch a glimpse of the third man as he passed between two buildings.

Jacob stood up and started toward the livery stable, his gun still firmly griped in his hand. As he came near the town folks, they stepped aside and let him pass.

He went into the stable and saddled his horse. To look at Jacob, you would have thought he was in no hurry. He simply wasted no motions. As soon as he was ready, he swung up into the saddle and turned the horse out of the stable.

Jacob set his horse into a steady, ground-eating gallop that would allow him to cover a good distance without exhausting the horse too quickly. He had an easy trail to follow. The man running for his life was leaving a cloud of dust in the hot still afternoon air.

As Jacob came around a bend in the road, a shot rang out. He quickly reined up and dove off his horse for cover behind some rocks. Another shot rang out, the bullet hitting a rock only a few feet from Jacob's head.

Jacob sat down behind the rock and drew his gun from his holster. He carefully checked it to make sure it was loaded and ready to use.

Another shot rang out, hitting the rocks several feet from where Jacob was sitting. He knew that the man was frightened, and probably knew he was going to die this afternoon.

Jacob patiently looked around. His horse was standing off the road in a grassy area. It seemed unconcerned with what was about to happen.

Jacob turned around and moved to the edge of a large boulder. He peered around the side of it and looked up into the rocks where the man was hiding. Jacob could see the man nervously looking around, trying to figure out where Jacob had gone.

Jacob took careful aim and squeezed the trigger. The gun jumped in his hand. He could see the dust and chips of rock fly off the boulder where the bullet hit in front of the man. He could also see the man duck down behind the boulder.

He knew he had not hit the man, but had only scared him a little more. Jacob quickly moved to another boulder before the man could see him.

Carefully, Jacob worked his way around the base of the rocks in an effort to get around behind the man. Crawling between the boulders, he worked his way up close. Jacob soon found himself above and behind the man.

As he leveled his gun on the man's back, he pulled back the hammer. The man had been looking for some sign that would tell him where Jacob was hiding, but when he heard the sound of the hammer set on Jacob's gun, he knew. He instantly froze, afraid to move.

"Put your hands up," Jacob said calmly.

Slowly, the man reached out and set his gun on the boulder, then raised his hands above his head. The man slowly turned around to face Jacob.

Jacob was surprised when the man turned around. What he saw under the cowboy hat was just a kid, maybe sixteen years old. This was the first time that Jacob had gotten a good look at him.

"Don't shoot, Mister. Please," the boy pleaded.

Jacob stood frozen, unable to believe that he had been chasing a boy. He just stared at the boy for several minutes, his gun still pointed at him.

"You killed my wife and son," Jacob finally said.

"I didn't do it, Mister. Honest. I was there, but I didn't kill no one."

"You were a party to it, that makes you as guilty as the rest," Jacob said as he tried to convince himself to kill the boy.

"Please, Mister. I tried to stop them, but they wouldn't listen," the boy pleaded.

Jacob couldn't make up his mind. He wanted more than anything to kill the boy for what he had been a party to, but he was just a kid. Killing a kid didn't set well with Jacob's way of thinking, although he had killed many boys during the war. If he killed this kid, it would make him no better than the two he had already killed.

His mind was in turmoil over what to do. One part of Jacob's head told him that he had killed enough. Two of them were dead, or soon would be. The third was standing in front of him, his face showing his fear of dying. The other part told him to kill the kid because he was as guilty as the others.

Jacob remembered in the recesses of his mind what the Bible had said about an eye for an eye. If he took it literally, he had lost two, they had lost two. The debt was paid. Even though it added up, somehow it still didn't seem to Jacob that justice had been served unless all those involved where dead.

As he tossed around in his mind what he should do, he unintentionally let his gun slowly drop to his side. He was so engrossed in his thoughts he hadn't realized that he had let his guard down.

For the first time, he thought about what he had done, and what he was doing. He had taken the law into his own hands. He no longer wanted revenge. He just wanted it to be over. Maybe it was time to let the law take care of the last one.

Just as Jacob looked up, he saw the boy reach out for his gun that was lying next to him on the boulder. Before it completely registered in Jacob's mind what was happening, the kid had grabbed the gun and was swinging it around toward him. Jacob reacted quickly, without thinking. As the kid's gun went off, so did Jacob's. The kid's shot went wild and missed Jacob by a good two feet, but Jacob's was on the mark.

The bullet from Jacob's gun smashed into the boy's chest, slamming him back against the rock. Jacob watched as the gun fell from the boy's hand. He could also see the fear on the boy's face as his life slipped away.

In a matter of a few seconds, the boy was dead. Jacob sat down on the rock and stared at the boy's lifeless body. He had gotten his revenge, but it didn't make him feel any better. If anything, he felt worse. Justice may have been served, but revenge had left him with an empty, sick feeling deep in his stomach. Killing the murderers of his wife and son did nothing to help him deal with his loss.

It was over. The only thing left to do was to take the boy's body back to town and let the town folks bury him with the others. He packed the boy over his horse and turned back toward town.

Riding up in front of the saloon, Jacob got down from the saddle. The barkeep came out as Jacob was tying the boy's horse to the hitching rail.

"The three men who died in your town today killed my wife and son. You can do with them as you wish," Jacob said.

Jacob took the reins of his horse, put his foot in the stirrup, and swung his leg over the saddle. Without another word, he turned his horse around and left town.

"What are their names," the barkeep called out.

Jacob did not answer. He couldn't answer because he did not know their names. As far as he was concerned, it was over. It was time to put it behind him and move on. It was time to try and put his life back together again, so he simply continued to ride on out of town without looking back.